HOMEFRONT

Homefront

A Story of Love and War

by

Geraldine Boyce

To my dear friend
Jo Anne
With love
Geraldine Boyce

FITHIAN PRESS, SANTA BARBARA, CALIFORNIA · 2000

Published by Fithian Press
A division of Daniel and Daniel, Publishers, Inc.
Post Office Box 1525
Santa Barbara, CA 93102
www.danielpublishing.com

LIBRARY OF CONGRESS CATALOGING-IN-PUBLICATION DATA
Boyce, Geraldine, (date)
  Homefront : a story of love and war / by Geraldine Boyce.
    p.   cm.
  ISBN 1-564764-341-1
  1. World War, 1939–1945—England—Fiction. 2. Mothers and daughters—
Fiction. 3. Americans—England—Fiction. 4. Weddings—Fiction.   I. Title.
  PS3552.08773 H66 2000
  813'.54—dc21   00-008373

To Larry

with loving thanks
for many happy years together

Acknowledgements

While writing this book I received much kindness from many people who are of generous spirit. My gratitude to:

Ann Lamott, whose book *Bird by Bird* inspired me to start writing.

Betty Hodson, and her College of Marin writing class, who set me on the right path and so much more. Her guidance and expertise were invaluable.

Jamie Tipton and his Writer's Center class for their thoughtful, supportive, and enthusiastic comments, so vital to any writer.

Marilyn Symmes, Kristin von Kreisler, and Cary James for taking time out from the writing of their own books to offer constructive suggestions and encouragement.

Anthony and Renette Symmes for painstakingly putting my initial manuscript into their computer, introducing me to the electronic world, and urging me onward.

Eric Larson for expertly editing this book with kind patience. And, finally I thank John Daniel, publisher of Fithian Press, for his courtesy while publishing this book.

HOMEFRONT

Chapter 1

April, 1947

THE DOOR OPENED AT 35 Hill Crescent, and out came a young woman, a girl still, running down the steps into the open garage alongside the house. She quickly turned her bicycle around, jumped on it, and pedalled off. Jenny Bartlett was late for the 8:30 A.M. train from Lansdale station, which would get her to work in London on time.

The sun had not yet risen sufficiently to warm the cool spring air, and Jenny felt the cold pass through her clothes as she sped down the hill. She prayed that the policeman directing traffic at Lansdale Bridge would beckon her through, as she often had trouble with her brakes when she had to stop suddenly. She was lucky and hurried through the crossroad and on toward the railway station. After chaining her bicycle to the railing, she ran down the steps and jumped on the train just as it was about to leave.

At last, Jenny thought as she sat down, I can now relax for forty minutes. She needed time to think. She took out a letter from her handbag to read. It had arrived the day before from Harrison Sanders, now back home in California, and he asked her to marry him. Jenny wanted to accept immediately, because she had known him a long time and had grown to love him; but before she approached her parents on the subject, she felt she should seriously weigh all the pros and cons and prepare herself for the objections she knew they would present.

Jenny thought back to when she first met Harry, in the spring of 1944, nearly three years ago. She had been invited for the weekend to the home of Marcia and Paul Hunt, parents of her friend Sylvia, a fellow student at St. Martin's College. Unlike her own parents, who led a quiet life, the Hunts often entertained servicemen from the colonies; but that weekend, for the first time, they had invited men from the USA.

Harry had arrived with three others, all second lieutenants. One was very thin and tall, and was from North Carolina, Jenny learned later; another was a huge giant from Texas; the third was a New Yorker, blond and very handsome—but "watch out," Jenny quickly told herself. The fourth was Harry. He was the shortest, perhaps five feet nine inches, with glasses and dark brown curly hair, like Jenny's. He was the oldest of the group, but he looked young for his twenty-seven years. He also seemed to be the quietest, for they were a noisy lot; but he was not shy. He noticed Jenny studying them from across the room and quickly went over.

"I'm Harrison Sanders from California," he said, putting out his hand for her to shake. "Are you the daughter of the house?"

"No," Jenny answered, "just a friend visiting for the weekend."

"Lucky that we've both been invited on the same weekend," he said, smiling at her again, and his smile, which showed such kindness and pleasure at their meeting, won her over to him immediately.

Harry asked her to dance as soon as the music started and immediately noticed two things about her: that her eyes were green, and that although she was five inches shorter than him, they fit together perfectly.

Everyone changed partners many times during the evening, but Harry kept coming back to dance with her, and when he left he asked Jenny for her telephone number.

Sylvia liked the handsome lieutenant from New York and after the party the two girls talked late into the night until Sylvia fell asleep. Jenny lay awake longer. She felt something important had happened, but she didn't know what it was.

When Harry phoned a few days later, Jenny's mother, Eleanor, answered in her clear English girlish voice, which made it difficult for young men, when they phoned the house, to differentiate between mother and daughters. When she found out who it was, Harry found himself being put through an interrogation, which Eleanor ended with: "Do you know Jenny's only just seventeen?" Harry knew Jenny was young, but not that young, and he understood her mother's need to be wary and protective. But when Eleanor added, "And you Americans have such a bad reputation," Harry felt obliged to answer politely, "Not all of us have, Mrs. Bartlett." To his relief, Eleanor said no more and Jenny came on the line. When she agreed to meet him for dinner the next night, he felt that her mother's "baptism by fire" had been worth it, and after the first date Harry was determined to see Jenny as often as he could. That was easy while Harry was still stationed in London, but within a month he was transferred to Bristol, in West England.

Harry found himself billeted in a small two-bedroom, one-bath row house with an elderly couple who were dismayed by the intrusion into their quiet lives. However, after having heard their neighbors' complaints about the men billeted with them, they assured him that they were grateful to have a polite, non-drinking man sharing their home. Partly to relieve them, but mainly to see Jenny, he went up to London whenever he could get a few hours off, until D-Day, June 6, 1944, when the Allies invaded Normandy. Harry and his unit soon followed across the English Channel to set up communication centers for the Signal Intelligence Corps.

They wrote each other often, and when the war in Europe ended on May 8, 1945, they kept on hoping that Harry would get one more leave in England before sailing for home. In September he wrote that he had been ordered to return to the US directly from France, and that he was very disappointed. Jenny also realized how much she had counted on seeing him too. So their letters had to suffice to keep the friendship simmering in the intervening years.

Jenny, deep in thought, looked up and saw that she had reached her station, and quickly jumped up and got off the train. Walking to the exit, she passed a row of public telephones. She stopped and retraced her steps, weaving her way among the throng of commuters who followed behind her. She put a coin in the slot and dialed.

"Southern Hospital," an operator answered.

"Ward Five please," Jenny said and waited to be put through.

In a moment a second voice answered, "Ward Five."

"May I please speak to Nurse Bartlett?"

"I'll see," the voice said, and after a few minutes a breathless Gwen came on the line.

"I thought you might be too busy to come to the phone," Jenny began.

"Jenny! I've only got a minute. What's up, little sister?"

"Harry's asked me to marry him."

"Do you want to?"

"Yes."

"Have you told the parents yet?"

"No."

Gwen sighed audibly. "They'll put up a terrible fight, but I'll support you, and I give you my blessing, of course."

"Thanks, you always do."

"I've got to go. Good luck! Let me know how things go." Gwen hung up. Talking to Gwen always gave Jenny comfort and strength. She'd gone over the arguments so many times in her mind, and she knew those in favor of marrying Harrison far outweighed those against. But to be sure, she decided to postpone telling her parents one more day; so when she got home after work that night, she said nothing.

The Bartletts' home was a two-story brick house in a quiet residential part of Lansdale, a suburb just ten miles up the River Thames from London. Having been built in the late Victorian era, it also had a full basement. All the houses along Hill Crescent were small; but as they were well set apart from each other, this gave a certain air of gentility and spaciousness.

Philip and Eleanor Bartlett had bought the house after they were married in 1923. Colonel Gowden, the Royal West Kent Regiment's Medical Officer, had watched Philip's progress from a sixteen-year-old private to a twenty-year-old regimental sergeant-major in World War I. When he returned home to take over his family's pharmaceutical manufacturing plant, Gowden Chemicals, he decided to offer Philip a job in the accounting department. Philip gratefully jumped at the opportunity. Jobs were scarce after the war, and he had already met Eleanor and was thinking of marrying her. The factory was outside the town of Lansdale, so when Philip began to feel more secure in his new job, that is where he and Eleanor began their search for their first home.

They loved the house as soon as they saw it, but the price was far above their means, and neither had a family who could help them. Nevertheless, they bought it and agonized over their incomprehensible extravagance, for they were both usually so careful and restrained. Over the years, as Philip advanced at thriving Gowden Chemicals, they "grew up" to the house, and neither he nor Eleanor were willing to consider that they had now outgrown it.

A large sign came with the house, affixed to the front gate, declaring it to be named "Adadene." And, as is often the custom in England, they were referred to by tradespeople, when making deliveries, as "the Bartletts of Adadene on Hill Crescent," never by the street number. A rose garden grew on either side of the path to the front door; and these had remained, sometimes battered and cowed, but always nurtured through World War II by Philip, who vowed he would not let the Germans deprive him of his roses. This had not been easy, for only farmers producing food had had access to fertilizers. But Philip had learned to sharpen his hearing to detect when a horsedrawn delivery cart came up the hill, and he rushed out with bucket and spade to collect any droppings that the horse might generously deposit on the road as it passed by. Sometimes a neighbor competed for the prize, but after a moment of annoyance (carefully concealed) the two men shook hands and agreed to share the bounty.

Philip, however, acknowledged the necessity to dig up the larger back garden to grow vegetables; but this, nearly two years after the war ended, was now restored to its original lawn and herbaceous borders. The house had also been repaired; its windows, chimneys, and roof tiles, shattered by bombs, had been replaced. Everything was now in the same good condition that Gwen and Jenny remembered from childhood.

Jenny wanted to wait until Saturday morning to tell her parents. This was the one day of the week when her father was home and the family ate a leisurely breakfast together, for on Sundays they went to church. The kitchen was where the family spent the most time. Jenny looked around the friendly room with its familiar blue willow-pattern china, now put back on the Welsh dresser which had stood empty all during the war, when the china was safely packed away in the cellar. During wartime, this room had become the family's center and haven from the dangers that abounded outside. Jenny was afraid her announcement would tear them apart.

"But you hardly know him," Philip exploded, caught completely off guard.

"You've only met him a few times," her mother chimed in. "How can you think that you know him well enough to marry him?"

"It's absurd," continued Philip. "You're still only nineteen, and you haven't seen him for nearly three years. You've probably forgotten what he's like."

"And America is so far from England, and California's even farther," Eleanor added pitifully, as fear of separation began to grow. For the family to be together, or at least nearby, was of the utmost importance to her. Although she was one of four siblings, she had been brought up as an only child by a childless but loving aunt and uncle. Her twenty-nine-year-old father had died suddenly from pneumonia three months prior to Eleanor's birth in March 1897, leaving his young widow poor and already with three children. And so, when she was three months old, Eleanor had been given away.

Jenny knew that her parents would react this way, and she answered patiently but determinedly, "I know I haven't seen Harry for a long time, but we've written each other faithfully and we both feel we know each other very well. I knew he was the one for me as soon as we met."

"It's entirely ridiculous," Philip continued, but the subject had planted a seed of fear in his mind too. He knew that Jenny could be very determined. Their older daughter, Gwen, was always much more amenable, even compliant, to her parents' suggestions. Jenny, however, always knew what she wanted and tended to hang on until she got it.

Philip and Eleanor later discussed "the problem," as they now considered it to be.

"I know both Gwen and Jenny have grown up early because of the war, but I've always felt that they're sensible. This time, though, Jenny's gone too far. I'm right, it is absurd," Philip repeated, "and I hope it all blows over."

The next week a letter arrived from Harry asking for Jenny's hand in marriage. Philip and Eleanor considered this an unfortunate turn of events.

The three of them discussed the matter again, the parents united against, with Jenny spiritedly putting forth positive arguments.

"Let's ask Gwen to come home," Eleanor suggested. "She's always such a voice of reason." Gwen was phoned to come home on her day off from nursing duties at the hospital in Oxford. She knew what to expect, because Jenny had already written her, and she dreaded it. There was nothing Gwen disliked more than confrontations, and she always tried to avoid them.

Gwen arrived looking tired. She had been on night duty all week. Immediately Eleanor was worried.

"I hope you're getting plenty of sleep, dear, and eating well."

"Yes, Mummy," Gwen answered wearily, "but the food's terribly stodgy, and I feel so dumpy." She was wearing her maroon tweed skirt, matching knit twin set, and the pearl necklace that her parents had given her when she went off to nursing college. She looked her usual slender self. Gwen was taller than Jenny, quite a beauty, also with dark brown hair. When each black-haired daughter was born, Eleanor, blond, and Philip, auburn-haired, were surprised, and Philip jokingly asked where they could have come from.

Jenny was happy to have her sister home. Despite the three years' difference in their ages, they shared a genuine affection for each other. Jenny loved Gwen for her sweet nature and for always being a source of warm support. Gwen loved her little sister for being so lively and spunky, a quality Gwen didn't have, especially when dealing with her parents. This time, however, although as supportive as ever, Gwen was envious of her sister's situation, for she had already met John Mitchell, had fallen in love with him, and wanted to marry him.

When John Mitchell came to an assembly dance a few months earlier in February, he had seemed somewhat out of place, for the crowd was much younger. He was already thirty-three, a captain in the British army, still in uniform. He had returned to England to be demobilized before leaving again in two months for Hong Kong, where a job was waiting for him in a British bank. On May 20, when John left by ship for the Far East, Gwen had gone to see him off at Tilbury Docks; then, later at home, she sat on her bed crying. Jenny joined her, and the two of them had sobbed their hearts out together.

Jenny felt she had a stake in the romance from the very beginning. The evening they met John, Gwen offered him a ride to the station. Since John was leaving the country again soon, he had not bought himself a car, and Gwen, having borrowed the family car, was obliged to take Jenny home too. While her sister and her new boyfriend sat in the front seats and chatted, Jenny sat silently in the back. After a while John invited Gwen to go out with him the following night, and she quickly accepted, but they could not decide where to meet.

Jenny was not sure whether they had forgotten that she was there, but after a few minutes of discussion with no solution, she burst out with a suggestion: "Why don't you meet at the Castle Hotel?" The couple looked around in surprise, and the matter was settled.

With the family together for the day before Gwen had to leave again on Saturday night, they thoroughly discussed the Harry and Jenny problem. They sat in the living room, rather than the kitchen, because Philip felt it more appropriate for such a serious discussion. After they all shared their views, Philip suddenly jumped out of his chair to announce victoriously, "Well, if young Harry thinks we're going to let you go alone across both the Atlantic and America, he's got another think coming. If he wants you," he added, turning to Jenny, "he'll just have to come over and get you."

Gwen and Jenny looked at him in astonishment, for it was unlike their father to be so emotionally emphatic. Eleanor, however, was pleased, for she could tell that Philip felt sure that this new obstacle would put an end to all this talk of what they considered an implausible marriage between two young people living six thousand miles apart.

But even this stand was quickly thwarted. Harry, an intelligent thirty-year-old attorney, had already come to this conclusion himself. Before he received Jenny's letter telling him of her father's latest decision, he had written to say that he was coming to England to fetch his bride. The idea had come to him one morning while crossing the Golden Gate Bridge on the bus to his office in San Francisco. He had thought about it a lot more while hiking the hills surrounding his home in Cascade Falls the following weekend. He wondered why he hadn't thought of it before. How logical it now seemed to him that Jenny's parents were fearful of her going alone all the way to California and the unknown. Harry now felt that going to England would reassure the Bartletts and clear the way for them to finally accept that he and Jenny would marry.

Philip had not left for work when Harry's letter arrived in the early morning post. He and Eleanor retreated to their bedroom, where they could discuss this new development in private. They prided themselves that they had succeeded in keeping the family closely knit, especially during and since the war. Now they were at a loss for what to do next.

Later in the day, as was her habit after finishing preparations for dinner, Eleanor went into the living room to sit quietly and wait for day to turn to evening. Dusk was her favorite time of day. Even as a child she had frequently crept into her aunt's parlor, which was seldom used since there were few visitors to their isolated farmhouse on the outer edges of Snowdonia in North Wales. Then, as now, she needed a quiet time to think without any distractions. As a child she had loved to dwell on the wonders and surprises of nature that she saw on the farm and later, when she was older, on the walks to school and to church in the nearest village of Cefn y Coed. She never felt it was a burden to walk the four miles to school and back each day and twice on Sundays, when she attended both morning services and Evensong, for these were her only contacts with the outside world.

But now, many years later, Eleanor felt she had more serious things to consider. She felt heartbroken over the possibility of losing a daughter (as yet she did not know of Gwen's growing affection for John Mitchell). One Sunday, while Jenny helped her mother prepare their big Sunday dinner after morning service, Eleanor could restrain her feelings no longer and cried out, "Why do you want to leave me?"

Jenny immediately went to her mother to comfort her and, putting her arms around her, said, "I'll never leave you in my heart, Mummy. We'll always keep closely in touch." But Jenny did not know the depths of her mother's anguish; or, in the selfishness of youth, she did not want to think about it.

Dusk came, then darkness, and Eleanor, hearing Philip come home from work, called out to him. He came into the living room.

"Sitting in the dark again?" he said as he always did, turning on the lights before he kissed her.

In all the years they had been married, Philip never understood why Eleanor liked to sit in the dark, which he found depressing. Viewing the now brightly lit room, he found it charming and cozy with its autumnal print settee in front of the coal-burning fireplace and the two matching easy chairs on either side. The room was sparsely furnished, for Eleanor could not abide clutter. But it pleased Philip that she had used all the furniture and paintings he had inherited from his Aunt Josephine. The walnut desk and chair were placed along the wall near the window, and the three small mahogany tables, two on either side of the settee and one in front of it, together with the Wilton carpet, gave the rather small room a feeling of spaciousness. Although Eleanor still worried over her interior decoration decisions, Philip felt she had succeeded in acquiring excellent taste.

After many weeks of being so sure of her decision to marry Harrison, Jenny began to have doubts and fears of her own. She wrote asking what had caused Harry to take this serious step after so many years of separation. He replied in his usual truthful and comforting manner.

June 20, 1947
Darling Jenny,
I began to think more and more of the possibility of our marrying last February when you wrote me about Britain's economic and fuel crises during an especially cruel winter.

I don't have your letter with me, as I'm at the office, but I can quote it by heart anyway. You wrote:

"It seems almost worse than the bombing raids of the war, because there was always something to do to help. Then streets were dark as a necessity for our safety. Now they are dark because there is nothing with which to light them. Trains and offices only operate in daylight, and there is little enough of that in winter with snow-laden skies. Many people have not had coal for six or eight weeks (we at home are lucky). Factories have closed, and the unemployed sit in cold homes with no power from 9:00 A.M. to noon, and again from 2:00 to 4:00 P.M. The three radio stations have been reduced to one, and they are not on the air till noon and from 1:30 to 3:00 P.M. The country seems to be dead, but I am sure my beloved England can survive and muddle through as usual."

This seems a cruel peacetime sequel to all the years of violence and deprivation of war. It touched my heart, and I became more convinced that I want to take you away from it all and have you with me always.

I talked it over with Uncle Ralph many times over lunch. He is a wonderful friend to me, and as an old romantic he constantly encouraged me to pursue the girl, reminding me often that true love conquers all.

And so, my beloved Jenny, that's why I asked you to marry me. I know it'll be a terrible wrench for you to leave your family, but I'm sure that we can be happy together.
Always your loving
Harry

Jenny hadn't remembered that she had written such a depressing letter. She had only intended to give some background on current events. She was completely satisfied with Harry's answer, but she still felt some doubt whether she could bear to leave her family, friends, and country.

If only we could easily talk to each other and hear each other's voices clearly, Jenny thought, we could share our problems and make decisions quickly. But phone calls between England and the US were quite an ordeal. The burden to phone fell on Harry because Britain's international telephone service was not yet fully restored since the war and the calls were very expensive.

Harry phoned Philip twice to assure him of his honorable intentions, but there was quite a procedure to follow before they could be connected. An international operator phoned the British operator to alert Philip that a phone call was to be made two days hence at 4:00 P.M. So Harry and Philip, at both ends, nervously waited for the call to be put through at the given time. Philip felt even more nervous because Eleanor stood at his elbow, anxiously hanging on to his every word to Harry, whose voice faded in and out. Each time this happened, Philip raised his voice to a shout, seemingly trying to project his conversation to California without any telephonic aid.

Things were no better when Harry phoned Jenny. Sometime only one of them could hear the other, so the precious time was taken up with, "I can't hear you," "What did you say?" and "Are you still there?" Often they were disconnected before they could say anything important. Sometimes Jenny ended up so disquieted that she wished Harry hadn't phoned at all.

The next time Jenny wrote to her friend Anabel Smythe, who had moved to Paris with her family when her father was posted to the British embassy there, she decided to ask for an invitation to visit them. Anabel replied promptly that they would be delighted to see her.

This was to be Jenny's first trip abroad. During the war, of course, no tourist foreign travel had been allowed. Indeed, travel outside Britain was still limited in order to restrain the outflow of money from a country trying to recover financially after a devastating war.

As she crossed the English Channel on the ferry to France, Jenny watched the receding coastline until it was out of sight. She tried to imagine how it would feel to be leaving England forever. She was relieved when the whole Smythe family met her at Gare St. Lazare in Paris. Mrs. Smythe and Anabel, both looking *très chic* in the latest French fashions, stood out with their blond hair amongst so many Parisian brunettes; and the family, just returned from a holiday on the Riviera, all had wonderful suntans. Jenny, with her pale face (a poor spring in England having followed a cold winter) and still wearing her old navy-blue woolen suit, felt wan and shabby. But Anabel's nine-year-old brother, Teddy, seemed so excited to see her that she soon forgot about it.

When the car stopped in front of a large house near the Bois de Boulogne, Jenny realized that Mr. Smythe must have a very high-up job at the embassy. He also had another car with a chauffeur, who often drove the two girls out into the country and to Fontainebleau and Versailles. The Versailles palace was still closed for renovations, but they peeked in the ground-floor windows and could see workmen in the long side corridors rehanging paintings. They wandered through the gardens, walked to Le Petit Trianon along the gravel paths, and admired numerous fountains.

Sometimes they went exploring by themselves in Paris, shopping around Montmartre and going up the narrow streets to Sacré Coeur.

Once on their way back home via Place Pigalle, they came upon a huge gathering of women and stopped to listen to a speaker who was shouting through a bullhorn. Jenny could not catch what she was saying, so she kept asking Anabel, who was now proficient in the language, "What's going on?"

"I think it's some kind of a union meeting," Anabel said, turning to the woman next to her to get more details.

"What did she say?" Jenny asked.

"She says it's a union meeting for prostitutes," Anabel answered in surprise.

Suddenly the meeting ended, and the girls were caught up in the dispersing throng. Numerous men, waiting patiently on the edges of the meeting, now came forward to make their choices. When Anabel and Jenny were approached, they ran off laughing, shouting, *"Non, non, non!"*

Mr. Smythe, a genial man, happy that Anabel was having such a good time with her old friend, invited them to the horse races at Auteuil. This was Jenny's first time at the races, although as a child she had listened to them on the wireless with her father. Philip enjoyed "a little flutter" on the horses himself and often placed small bets for Gwen and Jenny too, a shilling to win or place on the Epsom Derby or Grand National Steeplechase. The English were born bettors.

As soon as they arrived at the races, Mr. Smythe ushered the two girls upstairs into the grandstand, where they could have a better view of the course. They looked excitedly at the scene through their binoculars. When Jenny started to scan the racing sheet without much interest, she noticed that a horse named "San Francisco" was running in the second race, and she pointed it out to Anabel.

"You can't miss an opportunity like that," Anabel said as they hurried back down the stairs to place their bets. When the horse came in first and they collected their winnings, Anabel said, "It's a good omen."

"Do you really think so?"

"Yes," Anabel was decisive. "I'm sure of it."

So Jenny returned home from Paris having settled her doubts. Now she felt determined to follow her heart and go through with her marriage.

Her parents, however, were still trying to think of ways to prevent her.

"We can't consider letting Jenny go into a family without knowing anything about them," Philip said. "But I don't know how to go about it."

"What about Archie?" Eleanor suggested. "He's lived all over the world because of his insurance business, and he knows people everywhere."

Archie and Audrey Walden were dear old friends who never lost touch with anyone they befriended. After receiving Philip's phone call, they came right over.

Eleanor met them at the front door, and Philip, coming out of the kitchen asked, "What'll you have to drink? Whiskey and soda as usual?"

"Lovely," Archie answered as he went into the living room and sat down. Philip followed with a tray of drinks.

"The only people we know in the US are Marvin and June Ebury, in Chicago," Archie began, taking a sip. "I know that's a long way from California and from New York, where Harry's parents live, but I'll be happy to write them. Marvin's still in the insurance business, and he's been very successful."

The reply to Archie's letter was long in coming. However, two other letters arrived from America: one from Harry's mother, Dora Sanders, and her twin sister, Edith Whittlesey, who lived near Harry in Cascade Valley, a small town north of San Francisco. Because Harry had discussed the matter with his Uncle Ralph, his Aunt Edith knew about his intention to marry Jenny before his mother did. Ever a possessive mother of her only son, this did not sit well with Dora. Edith and Ralph had never had any children of their own and so were like extra parents to the three Sanders children, who spent every summer with them in California. And each child had stayed on through one winter as part of the Whittlesey household and gone to the local school.

Dora welcomed her sister's taking over some of her maternal duties. She wanted her children to know and enjoy California, for she, her sister, and five brothers had been born and raised in San Francisco. But she had not intended that eventually two of her children would choose to live there permanently rather than be under her watchful eye somewhere on the East Coast. When Harry decided to go into law (he was now an associate in Ralph's prestigious San Francisco law firm), Dora often repeated her regret that Harry had not stayed in New York and joined his own father's brokerage on Wall Street, and she never gave up trying to persuade him to return.

Both mother and aunt wrote extolling the virtues of their beloved son and nephew. They also ended their letters identically: "And we welcome dear Jenny into our family."

"All these votes of confidence!" Eleanor said rather prickly after reading the two letters Philip had handed her. "Although it's natural for families to praise their own, I hope they're not overselling the young man. But I wonder why neither of Harry's two sisters have written as well."

"Yes, I thought of that too. I hope they'll be as welcoming." But Philip was still holding out for an answer from Archie's friend in Chicago.

Archie phoned and drove over as soon as the letter arrived a week later. Philip and Eleanor waited anxiously for him and sat down quickly to listen as he read the letter, without their usual courtesy of offering him a drink.

My dear friends,

It's always good to hear from you. Jane and I often talk of the good times we had together in Australia in the 'thirties.

With our sons all safely home from the war, for which we are mighty thankful, it looks like some peaceful and successful years ahead.

I made enquiries about the American family your friend's daughter is marrying into. Do you remember Peter Coulsey? He was briefly in Sydney with my firm. Well, he's now in New York, so I phoned him. As luck would have it, he knows the father, Samuel Sanders; in fact they were in the same class at Wansworth College. Sam is highly thought of and a partner in a small but fine brokerage on Wall Street. They live in a lovely house in Steadsen, a good New York suburb.

Peter also knows the bridegroom-to-be. He went to Wansworth too. (In case you don't know, it's strictly Ivy League.) He is a fledgling attorney in his uncle's law firm in San Francisco.

So everything about the family looks good from here, but I wouldn't bet on any marriage these days. One of our boys is already divorced. Betty Coulsey finds the mother a bit sticky, but if the young couple plans to settle in California, this shouldn't be a problem. I hope all this gives your friend some peace of mind.

Love to you and Audrey. We'll send our usual letter at Christmas. Mustn't lose touch.

Yours
Marvin

Philip sat silently for a moment. He felt a sense of relief, but Eleanor felt anguished. She had been hoping for a negative report to give Philip some extra strength, since she felt he was weakening.

"What do you think, Archie?" he asked his friend.

"They certainly sound like a fine family."

Philip pressed him further. "But what would you do?"

"Well," Archie replied slowly, for he wanted to answer his friend truthfully. "It's a difficult decision, but I've known Jenny since she was born, and she's grown up well, which is a credit to the two of you. She seems older than her age to me, because of the war, I suppose...."

"But would you let her go?"

Eleanor felt tense. She could tell Philip was giving in.

Archie hesitated. "Yes, I think I would. It may be a terrible mistake, but who can tell? Before she leaves, though, I'd tell her that should she ever need it, God forbid, you'd send her the fare to come home."

Turning to Eleanor, Philip said sadly, "I don't think we can fight it anymore, darling."

Eleanor did not reply, but she wept inside.

Chapter 2

THE ENGAGEMENT WAS announced in the *London Daily Record*, and plans for the wedding proceeded. It was to be October 25, 1947.

Harry wrote that he would fly to New York and that he had booked passage on the *Queen Mary*, to arrive in Southampton on October 15 so that they could have a little time together before the wedding. Then, after the wedding, they would honeymoon for a week in England before sailing for New York, where they would stay for a short visit; then they would fly back to California.

The following week Harry wrote again. Plans had changed. His parents and Aunt Edith wanted to come to the wedding. Unfortunately, Uncle Ralph could not come because he had a trial starting around that time. Both he and Harry were disappointed, Harry especially so because his uncle had played such an important role in encouraging the romance.

Now the plans were that he and Aunt Edith would drive to New York, meet Dora and Sam Sanders, and all would sail across the Atlantic together.

Harry also extended their honeymoon to include stays both in England and on the Continent. Then, after sailing to New York and making a short visit to his parents there, he and Jenny would drive across the US to California.

Two more letters arrived from America, from family friends of the Sanderses in New York and California. Not only did they both send kind and glowing letters about Harry, whom they had known since birth, and his family, they also sent food parcels, which to a country still on rationing was a godsend.

"How kind," murmured Eleanor upon viewing food items that she had not seen in years, and she carefully put them away to share with visitors; for now she was resigned to the fact that they were going to arrive, whether she liked it or not.

In July, Gwen's Southern Hospital, bomb damage now repaired, moved from Oxford back to its original home in London, from which it had been evacuated in 1939. Since the larger London hospital could serve many more patients, extra head nurses were needed for each ward, and Gwen was promoted.

Her parents were happy to have her closer to home, only a half-hour away, and they wanted to set aside time to celebrate her success. They felt it was appropriate to divert the spotlight, which had been shining on Jenny for far too long.

Gwen was happy too, and after a holiday in Cornwall with friends, she looked forward to starting her new duties.

There was never any jealousy between the two sisters, each being content to be exactly who she was. Gwen only once showed chagrin amid all the wedding talk, when she confided to Jenny, "If John hadn't gone to Hong Kong, I'd have been married before you."

"Or we'd have a double wedding," Jenny answered in her usual quick way. "Daddy would have liked that."

Philip began to realize that the wedding was going to be a larger affair than he had initially envisioned. But he also knew he was a good organizer, and he was enjoying orchestrating the plans. As Philip became more involved, however, he did not notice that Eleanor withdrew more and more from the preparations. She decided that although she could bear going through all the proper motions, she did not feel that she had to pretend to enjoy them.

As the wedding drew closer, plans were finalized. Gwen was to be the only bridesmaid. At first Jenny wanted her two oldest friends, Nina Coulson, whom she had known since she was four, and Wendy Abbot, to be bridesmaids too. But it was finally decided from a practical point of view that it was unreasonable to expect Nina and Wendy to give up their valuable clothing coupons to buy otherwise useless red velvet for bridesmaids' dresses.

Harry chose as his best man Tom Harkins, an old army friend who was still in the army and who had just been posted for duty at the American embassy in London. The ushers to seat the wedding guests were corralled from the ranks of young men with whom Gwen and Jenny had grown up.

When Harry, Sam and Dora Sanders, and Edith Whittlesey docked in Southhampton, Harry insisted that he travel ahead of the others so that he could meet Jenny alone at Waterloo Station.

Dora protested, "Why can't we all go together? I want to meet her too." But this time she argued in vain. Harry was adamant. Dora had already succeeded in persuading Harry and Jenny to agree that she and her husband could return to the US with them on the *Queen Mary* (Aunt Edith planned to stay over on the Continent to visit friends). Realizing that his mother was intruding into their honeymoon, Harry decided to add visits to Brussels and Paris after their week in England so that he and Jenny could be alone for a longer time.

Colonel and Mrs. Gowden, Philip's boss and his wife, invited Harry to stay with them in their large house in Lansdale. The colonel had inherited his family's pharmaceutical company, of which Philip was now business manager. They had been together for a long time, during and since World War I, and he was also Jenny's godfather.

The Sanderses and Aunt Edith stayed in London. The next day Jenny and Harry were invited for dinner. Dora also invited a New York friend's two English nieces. At first Jenny was surprised that her first meeting with her future in-laws was to be shared with two other young women, the older of whom had once had her eye on Harry for herself.

"But in retrospect," Jenny told Gwen later, "I think it was better because it diluted the impact of the first meeting and it gave me time to assess the situation. Mr. Sanders is very nice, and he makes jokes all the time, but the twin 'mothers' are going to be a handful, I can already tell that."

Gwen was unfazed. "You'll think of something," she said, laughing.

The ten days before the wedding passed quickly. The Bartletts gave a dinner party in London for the two families. Dora and Edith both expressed their astonishment that there was to be no wedding rehearsal.

"How can anyone know what to do?" the two ladies asked.

"There's really not much to know," Philip answered patiently.

The two fathers got along well, which allowed Philip to feel free to broach a subject that had been bothering him for sometime.

"I've noticed that Jenny hasn't heard anything from either of Harry's two sisters," he began.

"Oh, really!" replied Sam, somewhat taken aback.

"I hope this doesn't mean that they won't welcome her."

"Not at all!" Sam answered quickly. "I know they're looking forward to meeting her very much. I guess they've been so busy with their growing families that they just didn't get around to it," he ended rather lamely.

While Jenny's and Harry's families were warily becoming acquainted, the two of them found time to be alone. They escaped by walking along the River Thames's towpaths, talking about everything, and they discovered that, different though they were, Harry being intellectual and Jenny practical, they were more compatible than they had ever imagined.

But even in such calm waters, a sudden squall often appears.

A week before the wedding, Harry, who was used to riding Aunt Edith's horse at home, suggested that they hire a couple of horses and go riding in Lansdale Park. Knowing that Dora and Edith were excellent equestrians, Jenny felt hesitant to tell Harry that she was not. She borrowed Gwen's jodhpurs and decided, with her usual bravado, that she could get away with it.

They mounted at the stables, and started up the hill single file. It was not until they reached the park and were side by side that they learned that the two horses did not like each other. After a vicious kick from Harry's, Jenny's horse took off at a fast gallop. Caught off-balance, she was thrown and, not having been quick enough to get her left foot out of the stirrup, was being pulled along the ground at the horse's fast pace.

As she was dragged over the hard and uneven ground, Jenny found many sudden fears passing through her mind: she was going to die, there would be no wedding, Harry was disappointed that she couldn't ride well, he would be relieved not to marry her. Please, God, will this horse never stop?

Harry, following in hot pursuit, was finally able to grab the reins and stop the horse. A shaken Jenny, covered in dust, released her foot and got up unsteadily. Harry dismounted and ran to see if she was hurt. They clung together, kissing.

"Darling, I was so scared," Harry said. "I thought I was going to lose you, just as I've realized in the last week that you're the most precious thing in the world to me." They kissed again, and Jenny suddenly felt confident that things were going to work out well after all.

She limped back to the stables, leading her horse, with Harry following at a safe distance. When Jenny got home she surveyed the damage. There were only a few scrapes on her backside, but Gwen's jodhpurs were ruined. After a good soak in a hot bath she seemed none the worse for the experience.

The remainder of the week was filled with frantic last-minute preparations. The three ladies apprised each other of their attire for the wedding ceremony. Eleanor was to wear a sage-green woolen dress, a brown hat with feathers, matching brown suede shoes, and her fur coat. Dora had chosen a two-piece gray woolen dress with matching shoes and hat, also with feathers, and a gray coat. Edith's choice was a black-and-white print silk dress, a white woolen coat bordered with black astrakhan fur, and a black-and-white felt hat. Each was satisfied with her own choice.

Nevertheless, in all the excitement Eleanor found a quiet moment to take Jenny aside to give her, as her own personal wedding gift, an eight-piece antique silver vanity set, engraved with her initials. As Jenny, touched by her mother's thought, looked at the four beautiful hair and clothes brushes, the silver-edged comb, and the three crystal jars with silver tops, she turned to kiss and thank her mother. But Eleanor had already moved out of reach in order to prevent any show of emotion, which was more than she could bear.

"This is something every English bride should have," she said rather brusquely. "You can't start your married life, especially in a new country, without something special from home." And she quickly busied herself rearranging the curtains before leaving the room. Jenny watched her go sadly, wanting to hug Eleanor, not only for her mother's sake, but because she needed to be consoled herself.

Jenny felt immense sadness that she was causing her mother such pain. She remembered coming home from school when she was little, and how her mother, always waiting at the bus stop, had opened her arms wide in welcome, and how she and Gwen would throw themselves into this haven of loving security.

Jenny knew that, for all her seriousness, Eleanor could also sometimes be surprisingly entertaining, even playful. The house was always full of laughter and jokes whenever her sisters or half-sisters came to visit. It was as though Eleanor was trying to make up for all those lonely years she had spent away from her siblings when she was growing up. On one of these visits, Eleanor suddenly came into the room dressed as Charlie Chaplin; but because Jenny, aged three, cried and screamed at the sight of this unfamiliar person, her mother never did it again. Jenny always regretted that her reaction had prevented Eleanor from showing this more daring side of her nature.

The wedding day dawned clear and sunny. It was a perfect English autumn day. As with most weddings, emotions built up. When Philip and Jenny approached the church at 11:00 A.M. in the hired limousine, Jenny, overcome with nerves, burst into tears. She suddenly felt overwhelmed by the gigantic step she was taking, which would separate her from the loving security she had known all her life, for she now faced a future where everything would be strange and unknown. Philip calmly leaned forward and said to the driver,

"Please drive on." He gave Jenny his handkerchief, and by the second time the car came around the corner to the church, she had recovered.

Inside the church, Eleanor stood and watched the procession as her family came up the aisle. First came the now-radiant bride in white satin and lace and her father in his morning suit, followed by the bridesmaid, Gwen, lovely in her long red-velvet gown, carrying a bouquet of yellow tea roses. Eleanor also glanced at other members of the congregation. What a wonderful yet bittersweet reunion, she thought. Seeing how her old friends were able to carry on with their lives gave her comfort, and she hoped that she, too, could face the future with courage. Among them were families who had spent happy and serene holidays with them at the English seaside resort of Whitney Bay before the war. What a long time ago it seemed.

Chapter 3

THE ROW OF SUMMER COTTAGES on the beach at Whitney Bay all looked the same from the front, but behind their facades they were very different. Two cottages had been made into one, and some had been expanded out back. If they had been somewhere else, they would have been called row houses, but all the people who stayed in them each summer referred to them as "cottages."

The cottages were numbered 1 to 14 and some of the owners had added silly names, carved in wood hanging over the front verandas, similar to names given by boat and horse owners. The few outsiders or day trippers who found their way there and walked on the public path in front would call out these names: "Bye the Way, Cuckoos' Nest, Bide-a-While," as they passed by. The path separated the cottages from the low wooden seawall, and beyond the wall a pebble beach with breakwaters went down to the sea, which was only thirty feet away at high tide.

At low tide the sea went out a mile or more, exposing mudflats where local and summer people searched for cockles, mussels, and small crabs. Beyond the mudflats, where the water started again, were the famous Whitney Bay oyster beds, with ever-watchful boats permanently anchored out there to scare off poachers.

The same families had been coming to Whitney Bay for many years, but none of them seemed to realize yet that they would not come again. It was July, 1939.

The adults in each family had chosen, in their usual understated English way, to ignore all talk of war. "After all," they said to each other, "we've avoided war before, and maybe we can do so again." In the depths of their own private thoughts, however, they really feared what lay ahead, but they were not willing to let this spoil their holidays by worrying.

Philip and Eleanor Bartlett always stayed in one of the smaller houses, Number 7, "Bye the Way." They had been bringing their daughters to Whitney Bay for eight years, ever since doctors recommended that the mudflats might be beneficial for the delicate Jenny. Whether it really was the mudflats or whether she just outgrew her ailments, Jenny was now a robust twelve-year-old developing early, and impatiently, into womanhood. Her older sister, Gwen, was of a lighter build and, like her mother, certainly of a more restrained nature.

Eleanor had always been a very caring, perhaps overly protective mother, but here in these familiar surroundings she could relax. Unlike most of the other mothers on the beach, she did not have a live-in maid, having only a weekly charwoman; but now the Bartletts brought with them a holiday housekeeper, Mrs. Dunphy, to do the housework and most of the cooking. The first year they had not done so, but Philip, ever watchful of the ways of others, quickly rectified this omission when he noted that other wives had help. Since tradesmen always came to the back door for orders early each morning, and deliveries were made soon after, Eleanor learned to relax about running the household. She now felt freer to play a twosome of golf with Philip every day and often a foursome with the Edmondses.

Philip, now a comparatively successful businessman in the pharmaceutical industry, was generally acknowledged to be a self-made man. He knew that the other men along the beach were better educated, and they were certainly better off financially. But Philip, at forty, was also proud of what he had accomplished by taking all the opportunities that life had offered him, and proud that his hard work had been recognized. He also knew that he had been lucky. He always worked to improve himself, and with Eleanor's help he had learned to speak in a more cultivated way, for she, with her gentleness, appeared to be more "to the manner born" than he did. In England, it was often said that a man's background was known as soon as he opened his mouth. While Philip was socially secure, he never missed an opportunity to imitate the good things he noticed in others. Perhaps of all the couples on the beach, Philip's and Eleanor's need for each other was greatest. Neither had parents or siblings to turn to, so they could rely only on each other. Philip often liked to try out new business tactics to see how Eleanor would react, for she had a calm and common-sense approach to problems. Eleanor, on the other hand, needed Philip's more outgoing personality to help her socially, for she was timid and quiet by nature. They complemented each other well, and this dependency succeeded in making them very contented with each other.

Of the six families who regularly came to Whitney Bay, only Charlie and Peggy Edmonds at Numbers 3 and 4 owned their own cottages. The other families preferred to rent at the time of year when the English weather might be best. In winter the beach area could be too stormy for comfort, with waves coming up close to, if not actually reaching, the cottages.

The Edmondses, who did not use their summer home more than two or three times a year, had transformed it into quite a showplace with all the comforts they had grown used to. The inner walls had been knocked out between the two cottages, making one large living room; the two front porches were glassed in to make a sunroom; and there were now four bedrooms upstairs with an ensuite bathroom for the master bedroom, complete with bidet. Charlie often unintentionally gave the impression that he had more money than he knew what to do with, and everything had to show. He had more homes, flashier cars, and entertained more lavishly than anyone else, but he was also a generous man, never looking for his entertaining to be returned. He just liked people.

Charlie inherited a chain of dress shops at age thirty-six when his father died suddenly. Now, nine years later, he not only owned those he had inherited but had added many more, so that he had at least one shop in every large town in southern England and the Midlands. He had also expanded his business into more elegant ladies' clothing under different names, so he sometimes owned as many as three shops in the same town, and he had acquired five clothing and accessories factories to supply them.

It was in one of his family's dress shops that he had first met Peggy years before. She had been one of the shopgirls, and although only sixteen years old, her striking good looks quickly caught Charlie's eye as soon as he started in the business. At first his parents were not happy about the attachment, having higher hopes for their son, but Peggy was good at merchandising, and with each promotion the family came to feel that she could be an asset to him. Moreover, the family realized that it was time for Charlie to settle down with one girl and stop playing the field. Although they had been sleeping together off and on for years, Peggy cleverly waited five years until the family completely accepted her, before pressuring Charlie for marriage.

Now, twenty-one years later, Peggy was still a beauty and, of course, the best-dressed mother on the beach and, indeed, at every function she ever attended. She retired from the business after being married for four years, to have her first son, Jack, now seventeen years old and then Billy, aged thirteen. During the years since, she had developed an almost insatiable desire to advance socially, so now Peggy spent her days attending charity luncheons, playing bridge, and drinking martinis, which were beginning to show on a fast-developing double chin. Because of her social aspirations, it was all the more surprising that the Edmondses chose Philip and Eleanor as their closest friends, not only in the summer, but all year round.

The Bartletts sometimes discussed the friendship when playing golf. The course ran parallel to the beach, just across the road at the end of their back garden. They could see the first tee from their upstairs bedroom window, and when it was free they hurried over to play a few practice holes before the Edmondses joined them for a foursome.

"Perhaps they find us relaxing and they can just be themselves," Philip said, hitting the ball poorly because he wasn't concentrating. Eleanor, a more careful player, waited to answer until she made a more successful drive.

"Maybe so. They don't have to prove anything to us." Then she added with a laugh, "Peggy certainly doesn't find me any competition in the dress arena." Eleanor did not care about clothes and was fully aware that she was not a smart dresser. Such things were not important to Philip either as long as she looked presentable. But they both had become fond of the Edmondses even though, as they often commented to each other, when Charlie and Peggy came over it was necessary to have on hand more bottles of gin than they needed to entertain any other friends.

The four children got along well too, breaking into partners in an unexpected way; Gwen and Billy started off together on their bicycles, then the older Jack with little Jenny, when she was younger, sitting on the back of his. It was fortunate that the younger members of these two families could entertain themselves, since the frequent bridge get-togethers of their parents brought them together often.

The couples' friendship started soon after the Bartletts arrived for their first holiday in Whitney Bay in 1931. It had a rocky beginning. Eleanor was shy and slow to make new friends and, in this first experience of becoming part of a holiday community, she was especially hesitant.

Upon their arrival, they discovered that the fences between their garden and those of two other cottages had already been removed to make a large grass patch for the boys' cricket games. "They play with too much enthusiasm," Eleanor grumbled one day when she rushed into the kitchen to find a cricket ball which had crashed through the window, dropping glass on her newly baked fruit pie, cooling on the window ledge.

As soon as the Edmondses discovered that Philip and Eleanor played bridge, they immediately invited them over for a game. No sooner had the Bartletts arrived than Peggy said, "There's a Jeannette McDonald and Maurice Chevalier *Love Parade* matinee on today at the cinema and the boys want to go with the other children. Would your girls like to go too?"

Eleanor opened her mouth to say "no" right away, since she had planned for the girls to play close by so she could watch them, but they had already heard the suggestion and begged to be allowed to go.

"Jack will watch over them," Peggy pressed. "What do you think, Philip?"

Eleanor looked over at him for support and was amazed to hear him reply, "Well, Jack's a reliable fellow, and the older children will be there too. I think it'll be all right for the girls to go if they all stick together." Philip was usually as careful and concerned about the children as she was. Eleanor could not understand why, with these new friends, he had suddenly become, it seemed to her, carefree and almost irresponsible.

The children left at 1:30 P.M. Eleanor felt disturbed by these developments, but she was not allowed to dwell on them, for she and Philip were immediately whisked upstairs to see the remodeled bedroom and bath and the Edmondses' latest acquisition. It had been sent over from America, by a colleague in the clothing business. It was an electric blanket, a new invention to the British and already working well on the UK electricity current. Upon returning downstairs, they were expected to admire the newly decorated living room which Peggy had just finished with her usual flair.

"You've done a beautiful job," Eleanor said, politely. "It's so much lighter than the dreary living rooms in the smaller cottages."

Finally, the four of them settled down and became engrossed in the game.

At five o'clock, when Eleanor glanced at her watch, she was shocked to see that it was so late, but she said nothing. By five-thirty she had become worried enough not to be able to concentrate on the game. Since none of the others seemed to have noticed the time, she timidly ventured, "It's already five-thirty. I wonder where the children are? Shouldn't they be home by now?"

"I expect they're on their way," Peggy answered, not in the least concerned. "I bid four hearts," and the game continued.

Six o'clock came and still no children. Philip was also worried and, realizing how Eleanor must be suffering, asked, "Where could the children be?"

"Oh, I'm sure they'll be home in a minute," Charlie answered. "Let's have another drink."

By the time it was nearly six-thirty, they were all worried. Charlie was as exasperated as the others. Peggy was comforting Eleanor, who was close to tears. Indeed, they were all becoming frantic.

"I'll start out to see if I can find them," Philip declared.

"Walk along the beach path," Eleanor called out after him. "That's the way they went."

After he had gone half a mile he finally saw them in the distance. Jenny ran ahead to meet him. "Daddy, we had such a fun time! We saw the whole program twice. My very favorite was when the big organ came out of nowhere."

"It couldn't come out of nowhere, silly," Gwen said impatiently, catching up with her sister.

"You're a fine one to be put in charge," Charlie exploded at Jack, rushing out of the house.

"I knew you'd be mad," Jack said miserably. "But as soon as Billy found out that the people in the cinema didn't know when we came in and that we didn't have to buy another ticket, they all insisted on staying through the whole program again."

Philip, feeling sorry for Jack and trying not to place all the blame on him, turned to his seven-year-old daughter. "You should have known better too, Gwen. You're the oldest. Your mother was very worried. We all were."

Gwen stood silent while her father scolded her, but she felt it was unfair. She always watched out for her younger sister and had today too. Halfway through the second show, Jenny needed to go to the bathroom they had noticed when they came in. After five minutes, Gwen, remaining in her seat engrossed in the film, realized that she should not have let her go alone and followed her. A man who had seen Jenny go into the ladies' room waited outside for her until she came out. He smiled and said "Hello," and Jenny smiled back.

"Would you like me to buy you some sweets?" he asked. Thinking that this nice man must be a golfing friend of her father's, Jenny was just about to go with him when Gwen confronted them.

"Jenny!" she said loudly. "You know Mummy always tells us not to talk to strangers," and she took her by the hand and marched her back to her seat.

Later, when they were going to bed, Eleanor said to Philip, "I was so surprised when you agreed to let the girls go. They're really too young."

"I'm sorry, but they were so anxious to go, and they had such a good time."

"I'm not sure about Charlie and Peggy," Eleanor continued. "They're too fast-paced for us, and I don't want to feel that I have to try to keep up with them, either socially or financially."

"I don't think they expect or want you to," Philip said thoughtfully. "Underneath all that bravado and show-off, I think they're two somewhat lonely people."

"Oh! Do you think so?" Eleanor was surprised, for it was usually she, and not Philip, who understood people better. She wasn't completely convinced, but she thought to herself, "Perhaps there's no harm being friends while on holiday." She felt that her authority as a mother had been challenged, so she added, "Well, I don't want to go through that agony again. I didn't even have time to remind the girls not to talk to strangers."

"We'll lay down the law, only one show," Philip said soothingly and laughed. "Sitting twice through a double feature, a Pathe Gazette newsreel, a cartoon, and an organ recital certainly does take time. But didn't you think the Edmondses' bathroom was very French?" They both laughed as he turned out the light and drew Eleanor to him and kissed her.

Chapter 4

THERE WERE TWO FAMILIES staying next to each other in two of the smaller cottages between the Bartletts and Edmondses. Ralph and Ena Thompson always occupied cottage Number 6, "Cuckoo's Nest." Ralph, a giant of a man, taught in a boy's public school in Warwickshire, and Ena, tiny in comparison to her husband, worked at the same school, in the office. They had no children of their own, but relished participating in all the beach activities. Ena once confided to Eleanor that she had miscarried four times, and now that she was of an age when she could try no more, it was a great consolation for them to surround themselves with as many children as they could.

The Thompsons owned a cabin cruiser, which they anchored forty yards offshore. They waded out to it, when the tide was receding, to go fishing or to visit islands scattered over the Thames estuary. Often, they invited a beach family to go with them. This invitation was not always received with enthusiasm since the cabin was small, and when Ena was the pilot, Ralph sometimes stood blocking the doorway with his large body and seemed unaware on choppy days that his guests inside were feeling decidedly green.

No one saw the Thompsons at any other time of year, but everyone exchanged Christmas cards and caught up on each other's news then.

To Number 5, "Bide-a-While," Mrs. O'Shea came every year

from Ireland, accompanied by her youngest daughter, Eileen, who lived at home and worked locally in Limerick. When they arrived in London on the Holyhead Express, they met the other members of the O'Shea family, and all traveled down together to Whitney Bay. It was always a grand reunion. Two daughters, Mary and Maureen, worked at the Board of Trade in London. The eldest son, Father Patrick, and the youngest son, Father Kevin, both lived in distant places in the north of England in lonely but growing Roman Catholic parishes. The eldest daughter, Kathleen, who used to come with them on holiday, recently married and now came only for a few days with her husband, English-born Terence Murphy. The other beach inhabitants wondered among themselves how such a large family of adults could squeeze themselves into such a small cottage. But they seemed happy to do so.

Father Patrick was a jovial man almost as large as Ralph Thompson, whereas his younger brother, although equally tall, was very thin and shy. All the sisters were quite plain and seemed to do nothing to improve their appearances; their hair was braided and twisted into "earphones" as they were called, which was, even then, a quite old-fashioned style. They were not prudish, however. They would enjoy a small glass of sherry, although their mother never would, and the two priests certainly enjoyed a glass of beer—or more—when it was offered.

One afternoon when Patrick O'Shea came into the living room he was surprised to find his mother listening to the radio. "Mam," he said gently, placing his hand over hers, "I thought we agreed not to listen to the news while on holiday."

His mother burst into tears, "I just can't help it," she sobbed. "If war comes, we're going to be separated for sure. I know Ireland won't side with Britain, and goodness knows what will happen."

"There, Mam, please don't cry." Patrick put his arms around her and tried to comfort her. She had always been such a wonderful mother. He was the second of her six children, and he was twelve years old when his father, coming home from work in the dark one night, was run over and left for dead. After he was found and taken to the hospital, he had lingered for a week before he died. Mrs.

O'Shea, her youngest child, Kevin, only four years old, had gone to work in a baby shop in order to earn enough money to keep her family together. That had been twenty-five years ago. As soon as each child could work, they all joined together in supporting her, and they paid for the summer cottage too.

Patrick, of course, knew well the implications of war, and silently agreed with his mother that Ireland would not become Britain's ally. That would mean no contact between the two countries, no letters back and forth, and even worse, no money could be transferred from the five O'Shea children in England to their mother and Eileen.

When Mrs. O'Shea went upstairs for her afternoon nap, Patrick called the family together to tell them what had happened.

Kathleen, who had just arrived with her new husband, spoke first. "It's just as well to have it all come out now, while we're here together."

"Not being able to write to each other will be so hard," added Mary, "but not being able to send money to Mam will surely be a hardship for her, and for you too, Eileen."

"Oh, we'll manage," Eileen answered bravely. "You've all been wonderful about sending whatever you could spare so faithfully every month. We'll miss it, I have to be truthful, but we'll miss your letters even more. Mam so counts on hearing from you," she said as she began to cry.

Each sibling gave his or her own opinion on the subject, and finally their youngest brother spoke up, quietly, as he always did.

"I've been thinking for some time that I should go back to Ireland and work within a diocese there. I've already made an application to do so, and I've sounded out old Father Quinn, who said he'd be willing to take over my parish in Yorkshire again. I think he's missed being as active in the church since he retired. I'm not like you, Patrick," he added, turning to his brother. "I'm really no good organizing all those youth groups and being an umpire at soccer games. I won't be missed very much, because I've never been able to become one of them," he ended miserably.

"Oh, I'm sure you'll be missed," Patrick said kindly, after a pause.

"We don't want you to do anything impetuous and regret it. Think about it some more, and we can talk about it again later."

The four sisters were silent and surprised. This was not a solution that any of them had considered, mainly because they thought Kevin was happy following in his brother's footsteps. His decision might be a solution for the whole family, but none of them wanted to appear eager or selfish. If Kevin was in Ireland, all of them would be much more relaxed, knowing he would be watching out for their mother, to whom he had always been particularly close. Both Mary and Maureen felt that they had good jobs in London and should stay there, and together with Kathleen they had begun to feel very comfortable in England, but they would not let their mother know this.

But still they had not been able to solve the problem of contact between family members.

"I've been thinking as you've all been talking. What about our cousin Daniel in America?" Patrick asked.

"How can he help? He'll be even farther away," Maureen commented.

"Well, we've always kept in touch," Patrick replied. "He really was the one who persuaded me to become a priest. I hear he has a fine, large parish in Boston. I could write to him."

"And he could be our contact between England and Ireland," Eileen interrupted, picking up the gist of her brother's thought immediately. "With America neutral in the war, we could send letters to Daniel and he could send them to Ireland, and vice versa."

"It would take a long time, but it would be better than nothing," Mary added enthusiastically. Patrick agreed to write Daniel that day.

Kathleen ended the meeting by suggesting, "I think it would be a good idea for all of us to give Eileen a check for whatever money we've been saving before she goes back home next week. Terence and I have been putting a little away in order to buy a house, but now who knows what's going to happen? How do you feel about it?"

"It's fine with me," Terence answered quickly, and the other members of the family agreed too.

When the two brothers went to Mass early the next morning, they talked on the way there and back. Kevin opened up to his brother in a way that he had never done before.

"You see," he explained, "I've begun to feel that I don't belong in such a small town as Upperdale. It's a beautiful area, but the harsh climate makes the people tough. The men, at least, have little time in their lives for church. They're barely able to eke out a living. Most of the people are Church of England or Chapel, if they're anything at all, so it's hard for me to go out and proselytize."

"That's what a parish priest has to do," Patrick interjected. "We have to keep on trying."

"I know, and I've prayed for help, but I'm just not cut out to do it."

"Are you friendly with any families in the parish?" Patrick asked.

"Not really," Kevin sighed. "I see Father Quinn once a week or so, but his only need in life is a bottle of whiskey. I'm lonely and isolated. That's why I feel more suited to doing the Lord's work in a larger diocese, with its ready-made traditions and companionships. I'd also worry about Mam if we had no contact, and I know she'd be broken-hearted. So to have two of us in Ireland would be a great comfort to her."

Patrick understood and agreed with his brother. "I realize that my congregation is larger, but even so it's uphill work to reach out to people. It's difficult to promote the Catholic Church in England right now. I find a lot of suspicion about it. But I have complete faith that it'll grow tremendously in the years to come. I have no doubt about it."

Kevin had been so frank with him that now Patrick felt he should share his own thoughts about himself.

"I've been thinking too," he said. "If there's a war, I've been giving some thought to joining the British army as a chaplain—if they'll take an Irishman."

Kevin was really shocked. "Oh, you wouldn't," he cried. "That would be like going over to the enemy. What would Mam think?"

"Well, I'm certainly not going to tell her until I've made up my mind, and that won't be for some time, as, unlike you, I haven't made any enquiries yet. I also know an old retired priest in the area, but I've no idea how he would react to coming back into the parish. Perhaps he'd consider it more favorably if I presented it to him as a wartime duty," Patrick added thoughtfully before continuing. "As for joining the enemy, I don't see it that way. We're all God's children and I, for one, wish that the Irish-English problem would end. After all, what would the Irish do if Britain didn't give us jobs, along with America, Canada, and the other colonies? We'd all starve to death in Ireland, and they need all the money we send back home."

Kevin continued to be amazed at his brother. But Patrick had not finished yet and continued, "Selfishly, here I am nearly thirty-seven, and I want some excitement in my life before I get too old. I think I'd make a good chaplain. Although I haven't personally experienced much in life, I'm not ignorant, even though I may be innocent. I know I can understand the problems of men, and if I could give faith back to a dying or wounded man, I'd be proud to do so."

Kevin knew he did not have the same ability to reach out to people as Patrick, and war was against everything he believed in. As the two brothers reached the cottage, they looked at each other, perhaps truly for the first time, shook hands, and went in for breakfast.

Chapter 5

PETER MARSHALL WAS A SURGEON with a practice in Serton, one of the southern suburbs of London. His wife, Janet, and his three children lived nearby in a large house surrounded by an acre of land. There Janet produced an abundance of fruits and vegetables, which she cooked and preserved with the help of her longtime maid, Alice, who always came on holiday with them.

The Marshall family had been coming to Whitney Bay for the longest time of all, and they always came to cottages Numbers 8 and 9. They were natural people, following the Quaker philosophy of frugality and kindness to all, and Janet laughed at her husband's innocent antics, for he was an affectionate, funny, and creative man.

The two Marshall boys, Jim, aged fifteen, and the blond, curly-haired, nine-year-old Barry, were like their parents. But their seventeen-year-old sister, Christine, was very different and free in her ways. She went for walks alone with older boys, not only from the beach, but from the town as well. Sometimes she sat on the knee of one of the fathers. Her parents did not consider this unseemly, but all the wives did, although their husbands, especially Charlie Edmonds, were more indulgent of it.

Each year Peter invented something, and this year he built what everyone considered to be his greatest success. There on the beach sat a sand yacht, shaped like a regular yacht, but with five large rubber wheels: two on either side at the stern, two in the middle, and one at the bow. No one at Whitney Bay had seen anything like it before. Peter sailed it across the mudflats with a crew made up of eager volunteers; Ralph Thompson and Father Patrick were regular and enthusiastic crew members.

Philip, who felt more at home playing golf or tennis, had never had the inclination or opportunity to be around yachts. He had always considered it to be a rich man's sport, but he reluctantly agreed to go out as a crew member anyway. The sand yacht soon picked up a good speed and, at low tide, it easily travelled the entire expanse of the flats. Philip, feeling the exhilaration of moving so fast, now understood why the other men enjoyed the sport so much.

Peter, the pilot, began to turn, and he called out to the crew as he tacked the sail. Philip heard the call but did not move fast and low enough, so when the boom hit him hard on the shoulder he went overboard. He rolled over and hit his head on the back wheel, knocking himself unconscious before he was run over by it. "Man overboard," one of the crew shouted. Peter looked back over his shoulder and jumped off the fast-moving yacht, rolling over the mud with ease. He got up and ran back to where Philip was lying prone on the drying and firm mud. He cradled Philip's head, lifted his eyelids, quickly checked him over for any broken bones, and was satisfied there were none. But still Philip did not stir.

Peter called out, "Patrick, Ralph, could you come over here and lift him onto the yacht?" The two large men ran over, and as Father Patrick leaned over to pick him up, Philip opened his eyes and woozily thought, "My God, he's going to administer the last rites, and I'm Church of England," before he fell unconscious again.

After the crew pushed the yacht the mile back to the pebble beach, Father Patrick and Ralph gently carried Philip up the beach, into the cottage, and laid him on the bed.

By now, Philip had come to. He was beginning to feel better and was embarrassed by all the fuss being made over him.

"I'm perfectly fine," he insisted. "I just knocked myself out." Peter checked him over again, giving extra attention to his head and reflexes.

"You're to stay in bed," he ordered. "You've had a slight concussion. I'll come to see you again this afternoon."

As soon as everyone left, Philip turned to the anxious and hovering Eleanor. "If you think I'm going to waste my holiday staying in bed, you're mistaken." But Eleanor, her nursing instincts rekindled, was firm. "You'll have to stay in bed today, at least, then we'll see about tomorrow. I'm going to do whatever Peter says."

The next day Philip pronounced himself completely recovered, and while Peter agreed he had been lucky, he added, "You really should treat yourself gently for the next few days."

All this had disturbed Peter. His life's purpose was to help people, which made him such a good and popular doctor. He could not bear to hurt man or beast, and his enjoyment of his new toy, built to give people pleasure, to his mind had ironically done just the opposite.

Philip did not really mind taking things easy, for he had not relaxed like this in years. He just lay there, letting his mind wander. He did not allow himself to think of the impending war, for he knew that once he returned home he would be immediately deluged with preparations both for his home and at the office. As a diversion, he thought of some of the foods he enjoyed as a boy. He remembered that he had often been sent to the fish-and-chips shop for chips. It was a huge treat for his family to have fish as well.

He ruefully admitted to himself that now that he had moved up in the world, he felt it no longer appropriate to be seen entering the fish-and-chips shop in the seedier part of Lansdale where he lived. The more successful a person became in England, it seemed to him, the less freedom he had. But perhaps, he thought reflectively, it is only this way for self-made men who do not want to return to where they came from. He decided that he'd drive down to the fish-and-chips shop later that evening and bring home a good feed for the family's supper.

Then he let his mind wander even further into the past.

Philip was not a country boy, although much of the suburbs of

London were surrounded by farmland when he was born in 1898. He was the oldest of his father's second family.

Frederick Bartlett, his father, married young and owned a small grocery shop in St. Mary's in Kent. Because he was an affable man and well liked by his customers, he could easily have expanded his business and become prosperous. But Fred was not ambitious, and because he was self-indulgent it became a habit to dip his hand into his own till and go up to London to the music halls. There he enjoyed the performance and the beer, treating his new-found friends to a glass also.

His young wife, Betty, remained at home, producing first one daughter, then a second and a third. She worried not only about the frequent removal of the grocery receipts, which left them short when they needed to reorder supplies for the shop, but also, each time Fred returned home late from London he was even more enthusiastic than usual to wake her up to make love.

Betty, anxious to please Fred in every way, became more afraid each time she conceived another child, which they could not afford. She begged Fred to be more businesslike, sometimes hiding what little money they had.

Betty could not count on Fred's two older sisters, Josephine and Pauline, for any moral support. They were indulgent of their younger brother and often gave him money to go to London when he had no money of his own. Possibly this sisterly indulgence stemmed from the fact that they were both good performers and sorely regretted not going on the stage themselves. But at eighteen the very beautiful Josephine met a rich man and became his mistress in a lovely home in Brighton. The more flamboyant Pauline, to everyone's surprise, married a subdued bank clerk. While certainly not as well off financially, she never ceased to remind her sister that her own wedding ring was, at least, authentic.

By the time the youngest little girl was three, what Betty feared had happened. She became pregnant again. This time, worn down by her peripatetic and ever-affectionate husband, she died along with her fourth newborn baby girl. So Fred was left with three daughters, aged seven, five, and three. Also he was barely eking out a living from his small shop. Fred's two adoring sisters, who never had or wanted children, did not come forward to help him. Indeed, Josephine had already left with her gentleman friend on an adventurous and elegant trip to Russia and was not to return for five months. Pauline did come over occasionally, and to the delight of her little nieces sat down at the piano to play and sing songs, bouncing up and down on the stool to emphasize the words, especially when they turned risqué.

Fred immediately started to look for temporary help for his little girls and a permanent replacement for Betty. Mrs. Baker, a kindly neighbor and already a mother of five, decided that perhaps three more children to look after would not make much difference, and a little extra money would come in useful. So the three Bartlett girls found themselves in a loving family setting and soon began not to miss their own mother as much as they adjusted, commingled, and survived the onslaught of the five Baker children.

Fred, although he tried to adjust to his own loss, was not faring so well. He was neither a natural husband nor father, and certainly not a businessman. For a while he stayed closer to home and kept his hand out of the till. His problems, as he saw them, were that he needed a woman to fulfill his own large sexual needs, he needed a woman to be a mother to his three children, and he needed a wife with money. The women he met in London would not fill all three requirements; instead they encouraged him to spend his money on them. So he decided to cast his eye closer to home. And that was how he came to think surprisingly of Kate Morford. He had seen Kate and her mother for years, walking by his house to church every Sunday. Kate was the daughter of the village postmaster, who was now deceased. He and his wife had married late, and Mrs. Morford was forty-two and he forty-eight when Kate was born, twenty-eight years ago. The two Morford women were tall and straight-backed, as were many Victorian women whose postures were supported by corsets. Mrs. Morford, now quite infirm, saw no reason why Kate should not continue to take care of her as she always had, and never considered her daughter's own feelings and desires. She presumed that Kate shared her views about the physical side of marriage, but, of course, they never discussed the subject. And Kate, trained to be the dutiful daughter, perhaps never allowed herself to think about such things.

So it was all the more strange that Fred, a short, gregarious, and even dissolute man, should consider Kate as a possible wife, but he began to give a lot of thought to how he could promote and develop a closer relationship. He decided on a particularly cold day not to send his delivery boy, Jim, out with the Morford order. He closed up shop early and delivered it himself. When Fred knocked on the back door, Kate opened it, saying in surprise, "Oh, Mr. Bartlett!"

"Who is it?" Mrs. Morford called out.

"It's Mr. Bartlett, Mother, with our delivery."

Mrs. Morford, not disturbing herself from her chair, and perhaps not able to get out of it alone, called out again, "Well, ask him in and close the door to keep out the cold," adding as Fred entered, "Is Jim ill?"

"No," Fred answered honestly, but he added an embellishment to the truth. "He had so many deliveries today that I decided to close the shop early and deliver some of them myself."

"How kind of you," Mrs. Morford said. "Kate, give Mr. Bartlett a cup of tea to warm him up." As he stood there drinking his tea, Fred looked around the neat and cozy kitchen with its shiny copper pots hanging on the wall, and wished he could stay there forever.

Kate was dressed as usual in black. Her high-necked serge dress, with its leg-of-mutton sleeves, showed the line of her bosom and her slender waist, which pleased Fred. Her tawny hair, with natural curls on her brow, was drawn back into a tight bun, and her unadorned handsome face, with its rather pointed nose, made Fred realize more than ever how desirable she was. He continued to deliver their groceries from time to time, prompting Mrs. Morford to comment, "I wonder if it's because he doesn't want to pay his delivery boy to do it?" Everyone in town knew about Fred's profligate ways.

Then one day she caught Fred looking at Kate in a certain way, and Mrs. Morford said to her after he left, "I do hope Mr. Bartlett is not allowing himself to think of you for his next wife, my dear. But, of course, you know all about the man, so that would be absurd." Kate blushed and quickly turned to wash the teacups in the sink before replying, "Of course, Mother." Kate, too, had seen Fred looking at her, and she had to confess to herself that she found the thought exciting.

But Mrs. Morford had sensed a warning, and from then on she did not offer Fred a cup of tea when he came, explaining to herself and Kate, "It's far better that he hurry home to his three little girls."

As the year continued, Mrs. Morford, who never went anywhere anymore, was persuaded by the vicar to allow herself to be transported in a rich parishioner's carriage to the church fair. And a terrible misfortune befell her. She tripped going up the path to the vicarage and broke her hip.

Kate attended her daily at the hospital until finally Mrs. Morford was allowed to come home and was carried up to her bedroom on a stretcher.

Fred decided to start up his deliveries again. After a few weeks, while sitting at her mother's bedside, Kate could see him coming down the road and would get up saying, "I'll go downstairs and make supper."

Mrs. Morford always replied, "I'm not hungry, dear," but Kate pressed her mother, "You must eat something." Then she slipped away downstairs, opened the door quietly, and let Fred in. This is how their friendship developed, and Kate found herself falling in love and having emotions she had never known before.

Mrs. Morford continued to decline in health, for her hip never healed, and she died in September.

Fred and Kate married in October. Everyone was astounded that this quiet, gentle, and ladylike person found in Fred, with all his well-known faults, someone to love.

At first Kate was extremely happy as a wife and as a mother to Fred's three little girls, but after the birth of her first-born son eleven months later, her marital rapture began to pall. Yet the miracle of her first child, whom they named Philip, after her father, never left her. Fred had hoped to name his first son after himself, but he had many more opportunities to do so, for Philip was followed in rapid succession by four more sons and a daughter. Philip was always special to Kate, the son who kept her spirits up when things got worse. Fred never changed his ways, but looked for even more excuses to go to London to escape a home crowded with children and, all too soon, an invalid wife.

Philip was a loving child, especially to his mother, and as he grew older he became more aware of the hardships of her life. Kate's own inheritance was quickly spent to support her growing family. As soon as he was old enough, Philip hired himself out to do any jobs that he could find, always bringing the money he earned home to his mother, who was now a sick and worn-out woman of forty.

When World War I started in September 1914, Philip, only sixteen, ran off to join the Royal West Regiment. His mother, who begged him not to go, was heartbroken. This was the only time Philip disobeyed her, but he was sure that if he did not join up immediately, the war would be over and he would miss all the excitement. As it turned out, for the entire four years of the war he was behind the front line in France. Every month he sent part of his pay home to his mother: half was to be spent on herself and the children, and half was to be put in his savings account for him to use when he came out of the army after the war.

As the war progressed, so did Philip. By the time he was twenty he had become the youngest regimental sergeant-major in the British army. He was offered a commission many times, and although in later years he regretted not having become an officer, he also knew he would not have survived. Young subalterns were sent back to England for a few weeks' training on how to lead their men into attacking the enemy. They were considered "cannon fodder," and that was how Britain lost a whole generation of men to war.

After the armistice in November 1918, Philip's regimental medical officer, Colonel Malcolm Gowden, was assigned to a military hospital outside the cathedral town of Salisbury in order to treat the dwindling number of acutely injured. Colonel Gowden requested that Philip go with him on his administrative staff. It was here that he met Eleanor, a nurse at the hospital, and fell in love with her.

The colonel, having watched Philip work in both France and England, asked him if he would be interested in working for the Gowden Chemical Company, which was owned by his family. Philip did not need to give the matter any thought, for he had no other prospects waiting for him at home, and he immediately and gratefully accepted.

When he was discharged from the army, Philip returned home to find his three older half-sisters already married and gone. His mother was completely bedridden and in a sad and neglected state. He wanted to move her quickly into a comfortable nursing home, but when he asked his mother for his bank book, she weakly answered that since she had been unable to go to the bank, she had given his monthly allowance to his father to deposit. Philip found that all the money in his bank account had been withdrawn, so he began his new career and his marriage to Eleanor with nothing.

Eleanor arranged for an old nursing friend who lived nearby to check daily on her new mother-in-law, who lingered in declining health for another two years. She was fifty-four when she died.

Philip sighed, then smiled. He could hear Gwen and Jenny coming noisily up the stairs to tell him what they had been doing on the beach that day. And he was going to enjoy his fish and chips!

Chapter 6

THE LAST COTTAGES FILLED with regulars were Numbers 10 and 11. Mrs. Patterson always came early with her Indian servant, Pashi, to prepare the two houses for the arrival of her son, Paul, who worked in the Foreign Office in London, her daughter, Valerie, and her cousin, Margot Jonkeer, who brought her large family from Holland.

The Pattersons were Indian Army types. Naomi Patterson's father was an aide-de-camp on the staff of the British viceroy to India, and it was there that she had mainly grown up, and she had returned to India after leaving boarding school in England. She was very beautiful and much sought after at the magnificent parties in New Delhi. But there did not now seem to be a Captain, Major, or Colonel Patterson, for the family never spoke of him. Many friends came to stay with them at the beach, some of them young women Paul invited, but they were mainly Valerie's friends with whom she traveled back and forth to India. Their frequent sea voyages indicated that they were part of what was called "the fishing fleet," those young women who, pushing thirty, sought husbands among the lonely British army officers stationed in India.

While everyone else became quite suntanned, all the Pattersons remained covered and pale. If any one of them ventured out into the sun without a parasol, the ever-watchful Pashi would rush out in his white uniform to supply one. Their lives also seemed to follow a more leisurely pattern; they were late risers, although with the seagulls swooping and crying over the beach every morning, they must have been woken early. Yet they returned year after year.

Margot Jonkeer and Naomi, although far apart in age, were like sisters. Naomi spent many school holidays with Margot's family—their fathers being brothers—when it was not possible for her to join her own parents in India.

Margot had met her husband, Jan, at the University of London, and after they graduated she had followed him back to Holland and married him. With her five children, aged seven to seventeen, she returned to England each year, leaving her husband behind working in his family's small manufacturing company. All the children spoke fluent English, except for the youngest little girl, Tania, who was deaf. She seemed, however, completely at home in the welcoming environment of the beach, and she was capable of getting anything she wanted by sign language, conveyed in either Dutch or English. The Jonkeer children mingled well with the other beach inhabitants. The oldest son, Willem, was, this year, particularly enamored of Christine Marshall. His thirteen-year-old brother, Till, played cricket with the Edmonds and Marshall boys. The two older girls, Sybil and Ingrid, aged eleven and fifteen, were good friends of Gwen and Jenny Bartlett.

Valerie Patterson and her closest friend, Cynthia Weston, a regular visitor to Whitney Bay, spent a lot of time walking out with the receding tide in deep conversation.

"I just can't make up my mind whether to return to India or stay here," Valerie said. "If I stay in England, I'll have to register for one of the women's services. I just couldn't bear to be a landgirl working in all weather. I'm really not qualified to work in an office, and I can't see myself working in a factory, can you?" They both laughed.

"I'm definitely going back to India," Cynthia said. "I feel more comfortable out there. I've been enquiring about passage, but all the ships are full right now, and there's nothing available until the end of August. It would be fun if we could go together again," she added persuasively.

"I dread talking to Mother about it and asking her for money for another ticket. She's already been so generous."

"I can't see anything but hardship here," Cynthia continued. "I think there will be fewer men here, too, when they all go to fight in France. It'll be more peaceful in India, with all the war action confined to Europe."

Valerie agreed. It did sound better. "I'll speak to Mother today," she promised.

When Valerie broached the subject to her mother later that afternoon, Naomi reacted to her daughter's request in horror.

"It's too late! And it's far better for us all to be together. You mustn't go back to India now." But Valerie persisted, and Naomi went next door in distress to talk it over with Margot. Naomi always discussed everything with Margot, even if only by letter.

"I know Valerie's lack of interest in working is partly my own fault. I've allowed her to grow up thinking of no one but herself." Margot agreed, but remained silent. She was constantly appalled at how Valerie expected her mother to continue to support her from a diminishing income.

"Have you ever thought to tell her that you can't afford it?" Margot asked.

"I know I should. Paul says I should too, but I just can't pluck up the courage to do so." Margot looked at Naomi earnestly. "Wars are brutal and terrible, but sometimes they present a person with an opportunity to choose another direction in life. Making Valerie go out to work—and in wartime they can use everyone—might even make her a more responsible person." Naomi smiled at her sadly.

Perhaps Naomi felt that Margot was less sympathetic than usual, but Margot had her own worries and decisions to make. She thought constantly that Willem would soon be conscripted; but the day before, something else had happened.

Margot was sitting on the beach having a nice talk with Michael Wisley, Paul's boss at the Foreign Office. He had come to spend a couple of days with the Pattersons, as he often did. They were talking of his bicycle tour of Holland the previous year and of the

Jonkeers' annual trip to Norway, where they escaped to be alone. Paul quietly joined them, and Michael turned to him.

"We've been having such an enjoyable and peaceful conversation, and now sadly we have to talk of other things." As Margot listened with growing concern, Michael continued. "With war certain to start soon, the Foreign Office is exploring all possibilities of how we can best defend ourselves. It is imperative that we have safehouses available to us, scattered over many countries on the Continent."

"We are wondering," Paul added, "whether you and Jan would let us list your home as a safehouse for allies to escape to or as a haven? We realize you have children and that they must be your first responsibility, so of course whatever you and Jan decide, we will accept completely."

"As an Englishwoman, I want to help in anyway I can," Margot answered quickly, "but you're right. Because of the children, I can't make this decision without Jan. I know Willem will have to go into the army soon. I can't see Holland remaining neutral for long, and if the war lasts, then Till will go too. But I'm also really frightened for Tania. She's so vulnerable." Margot became overwhelmed by all these distressing thoughts.

"I have to leave early tomorrow morning," Michael said, "but here's what I'd like to suggest: Let Paul accompany you home, ostensibly it will be to help you with the children. It'll have nothing to do with what we've discussed today, but he needs to get over there in an unofficial capacity so he can reconnoiter amongst our closest neighbors and allies." Michael sighed. "We've got a lot more work to do over there before the war begins."

Margot looked at Paul in surprise, realizing for the first time that he was a British intelligence officer. "I didn't know you were in this kind of work," she said. "Now I have something more to worry about."

Despite all the thoughts of war, the serene and relaxed routine of the beach continued. The two cottages at the east end of the beach saw a constant flow of lively theater friends squeezing in visits between rehearsals and plays. Marsha Cummings and Rupert Minto, two well-known actors, lived permanently at Whitney Bay when not performing in London. The gaiety of these changing inhabitants gave the impression of a continual party in progress. The three cottages at the west end had different people each year. In 1939, a honeymoon couple stayed in Number 12, and they emerged from time to time.

The Bartletts were always the first to leave, since Philip never felt he could spend more than a month away from work.

There were always noisy and rousing send-offs, sometimes with balloons or tin cans attached to the back of the car, which they removed as soon as they were out of sight. Peter Marshall, with his impish ways, was always the leader and instigator of new tricks. But this year there was no noise, only sincere goodbyes. Perhaps jokes were no longer appropriate because of the specter of somber times. So it was not until the Bartletts stopped for petrol halfway home that Philip found the "Just Married" sign on the back of the car. Eleanor was particularly mortified. "With the girls sitting in the back of the car as large as life," she said. But she laughed along with Philip.

After they settled back in the car they became silent, each preoccupied with his or her own thoughts. Eleanor chose to look back into the past rather than into the future, which held so many unknown fears.

But she found no comfort in the more recent past either. She remembered the first World War, the war that promised to end all wars. She quickly turned her mind from those terrible memories and reminded herself of the more peaceful times of her childhood.

After her father's premature death in December 1896, and Eleanor's birth the following March, her distraught mother, already with three children to feed, made the difficult decision to give her new baby to her childless cousin, Milly Williams, to bring up.

Aunt Milly was a loving and good substitute mother. Although separated from her own mother, sisters, and brother, Eleanor was happy and secure, a placid child, content with the quiet countryside and animals on the farm. When she grew older, the farmhands often called upon her to help them when a cow or sheep got caught on barbed wire. They said she had "healing hands," because she was so gentle putting salve on wounds, or attaching a makeshift splint to a chicken's broken leg or a bird's wing. So it was natural for her to decide that she wanted to help people get well too, and that she wanted to become a nurse. But Eleanor never believed it could happen, until unfortunate circumstances forced her to leave the mountains of North Wales and continue her life elsewhere.

In the late spring of 1913, Eleanor's beloved Aunt Milly, after a three-month illness, died of cancer. Eleanor nursed her lovingly, trying to make her well, but in the end Milly could not eat, and wasted away.

After Milly's widower, Robert Williams, overcame his grief, it became apparent that it would not be disagreeable to her uncle (indeed he was enthusiastic) to have Eleanor, just sixteen, replace his recently deceased wife, both at the farm and in his bed. Eleanor reacted silently and with horror to these developments. She did not know what to do, but she told her uncle that she would like to visit her mother, Alice Griffiths, to think it over. Robert felt sure that Alice, who had remarried and was struggling to bring up four more daughters, would see the logic of his suggestion.

Despite (or because of) the hardships of her life, Alice was a resourceful woman, and she immediately knew the right person to ask for advice. She took Eleanor to visit Miss Ethelwyn Markham, the headmistress of the grammar school which Eleanor had attended.

Miss Markham, an outspoken spinster from a prosperous English family, had chosen to come to this isolated part of Wales to educate its children. She could be seen in her heavy brown tweed suit, her pince-nez slightly askew due to the blustery weather, bicycling out to lonely farms to check on pupils who were not attending school. She was determined that parents, who often thought that farm chores were more important, would not deprive her students of their education. She fought for their rights, was broadminded enough to try to help them rectify their mistakes, and recognized genius when it was there. One of her pupils was to become a famous playwright.

Between them, mother and daughter told their story. Miss Markham listened carefully, interrupting only to comment angrily on the lasciviousness of men and say that Eleanor must, at all costs, be saved from the unwelcome advances of this terrible uncle.

"Do you really want to become a nurse, Eleanor?" she asked.

"Oh, yes, please, Miss Markham," Eleanor answered so earnestly that it was difficult not to believe her. Her old teacher remembered how conscientiously Eleanor had worked in school and how attentively and with such kindness she had nursed her aunt.

"I'll think it over," Miss Markham said thoughtfully. "But I do have a friend who is the matron of a nursing college, and I'll write her tonight. Of course, Eleanor, you're too young; I'm sure you have to be at least eighteen, but because of the circumstances," she added briskly, "we'll have to say you're eighteen, and I know God will forgive us."

Within the week Miss Markham received a reply from her friend Beatrice Abbot, matron of Northram Nursing College in London. Upon Miss Markham's recommendation, Beatrice wrote, Eleanor had been accepted as a nurse trainee for the next term, which was to start in ten days.

Miss Markham bicycled quickly to Alice's home to tell them the good news. And there was more. A full scholarship had been awarded for the concentrated two-year course. Eleanor, with Alice, returned to the farm to collect Eleanor's few belongings. An expectant Uncle Robert met them and was furious at this unfortunate development. Eleanor retrieved the twenty-five pounds Aunt Milly had secretly given her before she died. So with this money to pay for her train fare and any other expenses she might incur during her stay, Eleanor permanently added two years to her age and left for London.

Because she was suddenly afraid to leave home and go so far away alone, Eleanor did not question how all these events could have happened so fast. She never knew until years later that the scholarship money had come from Miss Markham's own share of her family's trust fund. But the schoolteacher needed no thanks. She had done the same for other students, and she was looking forward to following Eleanor's progress for the rest of her life.

The years at Northram College passed quickly for Eleanor. She studied hard, for she knew that she had not been as well prepared as many of the other students. Since she could not afford to go home, she wrote often to her family and Miss Markham. She was relieved to hear a few months after she left home that Uncle Robert had not mourned her departure any longer than he had mourned Aunt Milly's, for he was soon to marry another young girl from nearby.

On Sundays, her only days off, Eleanor was sometimes invited home by other students. Or she happily took a bus as far as she could afford to go (an allowance of seven shillings and sixpence a month was included in her scholarship stipend), and she walked on Hampstead Heath or in Richmond Park to watch the deer, birds, and changing seasons, just as she had at home in the mountains of North Wales.

Eleanor finished her course in the summer of 1915, and because of the enormous number of casualties among British men on French battlefields in World War I, an urgent call went out for qualified nurses. It was then that Eleanor was introduced to the horrors of war. She served in army hospitals in southern England, receiving wounded servicemen who had first been treated in hospitals in France, then shipped back across the English Channel. Eleanor, in her quiet, competent, and caring way, helped these men heal both physically and mentally.

Some army hospitals continued to operate after the war, because no permanent hospitals were yet available to nurse the wounded who had not recovered sufficiently to go home. Within a few years, however, this void was filled by the women of the British Empire, who collected enough money to build such a hospital for permanently disabled soldiers, sailors, and airmen. These women wanted a large, architecturally designed home with a view the men could enjoy, and they chose to build it on top of a hill with a magnificent view of the Thames Valley.

Eleanor transferred to a hospital near Salisbury. Soon after, Colonel Gowden was appointed commandant, bringing Philip with him as an aide on his administrative staff. Philip and Eleanor met when Philip made his rounds of the hospital to check on supplies. Eleanor noticed that Philip made more visits than were necessary; and she silently took umbrage, thinking that he believed she was not handling her supplies efficiently. But then Philip, now twenty-two years old, asked Eleanor to go out with him. Despite the thousands of soldiers who had passed through the hospitals where she had nursed, Eleanor, at twenty-three, had never fallen in love before. They waited two years before they married, after Philip settled in to his new peacetime job at Gowden Chemicals.

Eleanor looked at Philip as he concentrated on his driving, and glanced over her shoulder at the girls happily playing cards in the back seat. She always felt content when surrounded by her family. Whatever may happen, she decided, I know I've been blessed, and I'm thankful for it.

Chapter 7

NEWS ON THE WIRELESS confirmed their worst fears that war was imminent, and as soon as the Bartletts returned home, they began serious preparations. They cleaned out the cellar, reinforced it, and moved four cots down so they could all sleep when there were bombing raids.

By the end of August 1939, Britain was living in suspense, but many of the preparations for war were already in place. The Territorial Army reserves had been called up months previously, but now young men and women volunteered with patriotic fervor to join the three services. A civilian Home Guard was created to protect those remaining in Britain, should the enemy invade. Air raid wardens were recruited for each street, equipped with metal hats and flashlights, and church crypts and other large basements were prepared for their use when on duty. Bulldozers moved earth to build underground air raid shelters, and above each large city floated bulbous barrage balloons to prevent enemy bombers from getting close to their targets. Food, clothing, and petrol ration books were printed and, together with gas masks, were issued to all civilians. Although frightened by all these developments, the people stoically believed that their government had planned to protect them as best it could. War was now inevitable, and the most people could pray for was that it be a short one. It was always the hope that peace was just around the corner that kept them going for the next five years.

Eleanor bought and struggled home with yards of black material to make blackout curtains for every window in the house.

"Please don't walk over it," she said crossly to Jenny, who had just come in the front door, not expecting to find the hallway and living room floors covered with black muslin. "Can you give me a hand?"

They soon had a regular routine going. Gwen measured the windows, Eleanor cut the material, and Jenny sewed the strips on the machine.

"Do we have to be so fussy?" Jenny grumbled. "They're all going to be hidden behind the damask curtains anyway."

"Yes. We can't have any raw edges," Eleanor answered briskly, ever the stickler for perfection.

Philip had already volunteered to be an air raid warden on their street, and after attending training sessions, he and Bill Armstrong were elected to check each house to see that blackout curtains allowed no slit of light to be seen.

They were very demanding. "I can't allow our house to be sloppy when I'm telling everyone else on the street that they can't show any light," Philip told Eleanor.

Eleanor sighed, "We'll test them again tomorrow night."

But the biggest decision for the family to make was whether Gwen and Jenny should be evacuated to the country. All the children in metropolitan areas had to go, but Lansdale was one mile beyond the London metropolitan boundary, so decisions to evacuate their children or not were left up to the parents.

In preparation for the girls' departure, Eleanor took stock of their clothing needs. In her usual frugal way, she decided that only their nightclothes and underwear were in need of replacement. She took the two girls with her when she went shopping as Gwen, at age fifteen, had developed her own taste and style. Jenny, aged twelve, however, was still content to have her mother decide for her.

Philip and Eleanor continued to agonize over their decision.

Eleanor wrote her cousin, Mary Wilson, a spinster who lived in the Cotswolds, asking if she would take the girls. Mary answered enthusiastically that she would be delighted to fill her two spare bedrooms with such nice girls, whom she knew. Her alternative, she explained, was to be assigned two or three children from anywhere in London, and this was not an experience to which she was looking forward.

"We don't want to go," Gwen burst out uncharacteristically. "I'm too old to go, and we're both willing to take our chances staying here together as a family. We'd worry terribly about the two of you if we went."

Her parents were surprised at the adamancy of Gwen's stand, but they were also relieved and the matter was settled. They decided that the girls should sleep in the cellar so they would not be disturbed if a siren went off in the middle of the night. Gwen slept there until she left home three years later, and Jenny did not sleep in her own bedroom for the nearly six years of the war.

Mary Wilson was the only one disappointed by the decision. As she feared, she had billeted in her clean, charming, and exquisitely furnished cottage four evacuees: two ten-year-old boys and a young mother with a new baby. All were from the East End of London, had never been to the country before, and had never seen a live cow or sheep. They found the quietness of the countryside unreal and boring after only knowing the noise, excitement, dirt, and violence of the London streets.

"Poor Mary," Eleanor exclaimed after reading her letter aloud, "I bet she's wondering how she'll survive."

"The East End can be such a rough place," Philip added sympathetically. "I bet those boys will be little ruffians."

The Bartlett family, along with most other families all over Great Britain, gathered around their wireless at 11:15 A.M. on Sunday, September 3, to hear the prime minister, Mr. Neville Chamberlain, tell them that war had been declared.

When the speech ended, the four Bartletts continued to sit quietly, none of them speaking or showing any emotion. The street outside was deserted and silent. Everyone realized that the worst had happened: no longer could they harbor any illusions that the Germans would back down at the last minute.

"Well, I'd better be off," Philip said, getting up slowly and sadly from his chair. "Since I live the closest, I promised to go and check over the factory as soon as war was declared."

He went out the door and walked toward his car, then changed his mind, thinking he'd better walk to the office from now on to save petrol.

Within a few minutes the air raid siren sounded. The three of them left at home were petrified. Eleanor also felt distraught about Philip walking to the office, but she controlled her fears quickly in order to set an example.

"Get your gas masks and go down to the cellar," she ordered, following the girls down the steps, then asked sharply, "Gwen, where are you going?" as Gwen turned around and ran back up the steps. "To fetch Dicky Bird," she called out, and soon returned carrying the canary in his cage.

"I think we should put our gas masks on," Eleanor said, not knowing what else to do. Sitting there on her cot, she tried to calm herself. Things were happening so fast that there had been no time to adjust. She couldn't see well without her glasses, which she had removed to put on her mask. She picked up the cardboard carrying box with its long, leather shoulder strap. "It's going to be a nuisance to have to take this everywhere," she thought, but with her usual practical bent, she decided that it was large enough for her to squeeze in snacks for the girls when they were delayed by air raids coming home from school on the bus. Even this small decision seemed to make her more able to cope.

After ten minutes of talking to each other in muffled voices and peering through the clear visor at each other, Eleanor signaled to Gwen and Jenny to take off the masks.

"I don't think we have to sit here all the time wearing them, they smell so rubbery," she said. "If there's any poison gas, Dicky Bird will be the first to keel over and warn us."

Both girls, already overwrought from the day's developments, burst into tears and wailed at the thought that such an end could befall their beloved canary. But before things could get further out of hand, the "all clear" sounded. It had been a false alarm.

Eleanor immediately threw herself into volunteer work. When

her good friend Margaret Rogers, the vicar's wife, started a Red Cross group to knit gloves, scarves, and Balaclava helmets for servicemen, Eleanor enthusiastically joined. Then Margaret, always full of energy, set up a depot at the church, and again Eleanor agreed to help collect and sort clothes to give to the refugees who were pouring into Britain from countries across the English Channel. Already 55,000 refugees had arrived from Germany and Austria, 13,000 of whom were children who had come alone. When the total rose to 63,000, the British government set aside one million and a quarter pounds to pay for them to settle, but help was also needed from volunteer groups to supply clothes and household goods.

"I'm not ready to give that coat away yet, Mummy," Jenny complained, seeing her mother take it out of her closet.

"Now don't be selfish, Jenny," Eleanor replied determinedly. "When we have something, we should share it." And she energetically continued to clear out the closets and cupboards. It was a generous philosophy she practiced throughout the war, but her family reminded her, as the war went on and on, that they eventually had need themselves of many of the things she had donated.

Eleanor was never too busy, except on Red Cross and Refugee Relief days, to read the paper from start to finish each morning after the family had gone and before she washed the breakfast dishes. When she came to the obituaries on September 10, she read with shock and sadness:

PATTERSON. On September 3, 1939, torpedoed in the Bay of Biscay, and lost with all others on board S.S. *Clarion*, Valerie Margot Patterson, adored daughter of Mrs. Naomi Patterson, and beloved sister of Paul. Aged 27 years.

This was their first casualty of the war. Eleanor got up and phoned Janet Marshall and Peggy Edmonds. Both had seen the notice, and the three of them agreed that each of them would write to Naomi. They all received printed notes in reply, but Naomi sent no personal message.

The day after the *Clarion* sank, German U-boats torpedoed another passenger ship, the S.S. *Athenia*, sailing from Liverpool for Montreal. There were 300 American passengers on board, twenty-eight of whom were among the 112 who perished. Within a month, the aircraft carrier *Courageous* went down in the Bristol Channel with 500 lost, followed by the *Royal Oak* at anchor in Scapa Flow, Scotland, losing 786 men.

While U-boats searched the seas relentlessly throughout the war, the Allies also had reciprocal sinking "successes." The Germans stalked merchant marine ships in convoy as well as warships, presuming that if they could prevent food supplies from reaching the British Isles, the country could be starved into submission. Knowing these dangers, the British were grateful for whatever supplies they could get. However, they often sighed at the monotony of their diet; six months of only mutton in the butchers' shops, followed by six months of pork.

After waiting three weeks, Eleanor phoned to ask if she could call on Naomi. Pashi answered the phone in his clipped, slightly accented English.

"Madam is shattered," he told her, "and she is too frightened to stay in London with these incendiary bombs raining down on us every night. When a building burned to the ground on our street last week, she decided to take a house in the country, in Buckinghamshire. We're closing up the flat and moving next week."

"What about Mr. Paul?" Eleanor asked.

"He's sharing a flat with a friend and will remain in London."

"You will let us know how you're getting along, won't you?" Eleanor said, and Pashi promised he would.

Naomi was in tremendous despair because she felt that she had been instrumental in causing her daughter's death. If only she had listened to Paul and Margot and not given Valerie the money for her ship passage, she would still be alive. Naomi now knew that she had been a far too weak and indulgent mother, and the realization shattered her.

Chapter 8

THE EDMONDSES WERE ALWAYS the last family to leave Whitney Bay. As owners of their cottage, they had many duties to perform to ensure that it was securely closed up. They watched with envy as the other families just handed over the keys to the rental agent and quickly drove off. But each year Charlie and Peggy reassured each other how lucky they were, since they were the only ones who could come back any time they wanted. They only returned, however, for one long weekend in autumn. Once they had spent Christmas at the beach, but it had not been a success. The weather had been ferocious and the family had felt uneasy being in the only house occupied in the long row of cottages.

"We'd better do a good job of closing up the house," Charlie said. "We may not be back for a long time."

"Don't you think we'll be coming for our usual weekend in October?" Peggy asked.

"I doubt it," Charlie sounded gloomy. "I hear that once war is declared, they plan to put huge rolls of barbed wire all along the coastline of Britain."

"You mean we won't be able to swim in the sea, Dad?" Billy asked.

"That's right!" replied his father. "We won't be able to do a lot of things that we've always taken for granted."

They packed the luggage in the car and all climbed into the

Daimler, with Phoebe, the maid, and the two boys sitting in the back. Charlie was a fast driver (Philip considered him to be a dangerously fast driver), but his own family was used to it. Within two hours they were home.

As usual, Charlie outdid everyone else and built a whole underground apartment shelter at the bottom of the garden. It was magnificent. To enter they went down five steps and through a strong metal door opening into a living-dining room. There were two small bedrooms, a bathroom, and well-equipped kitchen with three hotplates but no oven. Hot water as well as cold came out of the taps, and there were electric lights, but in case of emergencies there were also extra lamps and a camp stove. Except for the lack of windows, many people might have found it a comfortable permanent home.

As soon as the shelter was finished, Charlie turned his mind to his shops. He knew it would be hard to get help in wartime. The usual supply of sixteen-year-old school-leavers for sales clerks would dry up as soon as they were called for national service. Perhaps he could get some mothers of school-age children to come in as part-timers. He had already moved on a plan conceived while sitting on the beach at Whitney Bay. He had converted three of his five women's clothing factories to making men's and women's service uniforms. This would be his war effort, he assured himself, feeling doubly satisfied because he knew he would also make a lot of money from these new ventures.

Peggy, on the other hand, was not taking well to war. She seemed to take it as a personal affront that she was losing all those things that she had worked so hard to acquire. First, Phoebe, who had been with them ever since Billy was born, decided she wanted the excitement of working in a munitions factory while earning more money. Peggy offered her a higher salary to stay, but Phoebe was adamant and moved back home with her parents as soon as her two brothers were called into the army.

Peggy also discovered that her friends were caught up in volunteering for the war effort, so were less available to play bridge with her.

She also felt it a terrible imposition that she had to queue a long time for food and that rations were so small after all the waiting. Because she had always been such a good customer at the bakery, a special cake was put aside for her each week, and Peggy felt somewhat comforted by the gesture, even though, of course, she had to give up food coupons for it. She was lucky, she realized, that the gardener, Mr. Wiggins, continued to come two days weekly, but she had never known how much time Phoebe spent running out to supply him with his morning coffee and his cups of tea in the afternoon. Often Peggy phoned Eleanor to regale her with her thoughts on the hardships of war, and Eleanor quickly maneuvered the hand-held telephone receiver between her head and her shoulder so she could knit while she listened. After a ten-minute conversation Eleanor interrupted with, "So good to hear from you, dear, but I think we'd better get off the phone, as the telephone company has asked us not to tie up the lines for long."

The two families visited each other when they could, and while sitting down to tea after viewing the Edmondses' newest underground addition, Jack turned to Philip and said, "I'm going to join the RAF as soon as I'm old enough."

"You're going to stay in school until your eighteen," his mother answered sharply.

"Well, *then* I'm going to go, Mother. All the other fellows in my class are going."

Eleanor looked over at Peggy, understanding her fears, but the two men understood why he wanted to go. Philip remembered how anxious he had been not to miss anything in the First World War. This time he was exempt from service because the pharmaceutical industry was listed as essential. He could not tell this to Eleanor, because she would never understand, but when their neighbor, Colonel Adams, paraded in Lansdale Park before going to France with the Royal East Regiment, Philip grieved not to be going with them.

"Did you hear about the mine washing up on the beach at Whitney Bay?" Charlie asked, anxious to change the subject.

"No, was there much damage?" Philip asked.

"Lots! It broke up the breakwaters at the end of the beach, but no one was hurt. Our caretaker said everything was all right at our house."

"Miserable things," Philip said, "floating out there on the sea waiting to touch something and explode. It'd be terrible if one floated into a harbor full of ships."

"I think they have some sort of barrier to prevent that," Charlie said. "You have to be impressed by all these clever young Brits; no sooner do the Germans invent a new weapon than they discover a way to counteract it."

"It's remarkable what they can do nowadays," Philip agreed. "I hear they've discovered how to make coal into steel and fats into explosives. What'll they think of next?"

"And they're making plastics for planes from milk," Jack said, joining in the conversation enthusiastically, "and turning potatoes into alcohol for motor spirits."

The men continued to talk about the inventions of war. Peggy and Eleanor said nothing; they were still dwelling on the emotional impact of Jack's joining the air force.

"Wonderful shelter," Philip commented as they were driving home.

"Yes, it really was quite palatial," Eleanor agreed, then added in her usual down-to-earth way, "but I doubt that it's any safer than our reinforced basement. A direct hit and they'll be gone like the rest of us."

Chapter 9

CHRISTMAS 1939 CAME with the usual exchange of cards. Eleanor was glad that the war had not broken the chain of communication, especially with those from Whitney Bay.

In her note, Ena Thompson wrote,

> Ralph is working particularly hard in school, adding new classes to his teaching load to fill in for some of the younger teachers who either volunteered or were called back into the services.

Kathleen O'Shea Murphy wrote for the whole family,

> It was a sad parting in London after our holiday, but one good thing is that just before war broke out, Kevin was suddenly recalled to the Diocese of Cork, so that's a big help to Mam and Eileen to have him in Ireland.
>
> Mary and Maureen have been evacuated to government offices in St. Ann's in Lancashire. I miss them terribly, but it does make it easier for them to see Patrick, still in his parish in Yorkshire.
>
> As for Terence and me, he was called up to the army in November and is stationed 'somewhere in England.' I'm still working in the insurance business in St. Albans, hoping he can come home for Christmas.

Although very infrequent, we are grateful to get news of our family in Ireland via our cousin Father Daniel in America, and we hope they get ours.

They received a card from Naomi Patterson, with just her name on it. Eleanor compared signatures with previous years and suspected Pashi had sent it. It was a wonder to have heard at all.

A few days after Christmas the Jonkeer's card arrived from Holland. Margot wrote, "Apologies for being late, but Jan and I worked especially hard on Christmas this year, as we wanted it to be a particularly good one for the whole family. Willem leaves for the army on January 3, his eighteenth birthday, and we may not be together again for a long time.

"I can hardly bear to write about the loss of my cousin Valerie. I am haunted by the fact that if she hadn't left England, she would still be alive. Naomi is, of course, completely shattered, and with no travel abroad allowed I wasn't able to come over to England to comfort her. I do hear from Paul quite often, and because of this tragedy we have become more like brother and sister than cousins."

There was also little peace in the Marshall household over the holidays. Peter and Janet were shocked when their seventeen-year-old daughter, Christine, announced in November that she wanted to join the Women's Royal Naval Service (WRENS) as soon as she was eighteen in December.

"Oh, you can't do that dear," her mother answered quickly.

"Why not?" Christine demanded, immediately on the offensive.

"Well, dear," Peter answered patiently, "we're Quakers, and you know that we don't believe in war. If ever a Quaker goes onto a battlefield, we go unarmed to help and carry the wounded to safety. Anyway, you have an exemption from war duty."

"What do you mean?" Christine demanded again.

"When you came to work in my office in September, I applied for an exemption for you, as is our right in a medical office," her father explained.

"How could you do that without telling me?" Christine asked angrily.

"The work is too much for Miss Ogilvy, and now that Mrs. Pierce has left to have her baby, I need you to help her." Her mother nodded in agreement.

Christine was furious. This is not what she had planned at all. She felt she needed to get away from home, and the war gave her an opportunity to do so. She decided to bide her time, and on December 20, her eighteenth birthday, she enlisted. When she broke the news to her parents, they were sorely perplexed. Christmas was a somber time.

"Where have we gone wrong?" Janet asked Peter in distress. Not having recognized the warning signs over the years, they could not understand how Christine had changed and become rebellious.

She left for Portsmouth on January 10, by which time her parents, in their usual loving way, had accepted her decision.

On May 10, 1940, Winston Churchill became prime minister, and three days later he gave his "Blood, Sweat, and Tears" speech to thunderous support in Parliament, *and* he formed a coalition government. Britain was in good hands.

Soon after, Germany invaded Holland and Belgium, following their occupation of Norway and Denmark. People in England worried about their Dutch friends, the Jonkeer family, and Eleanor repeatedly phoned Paul Patterson in London to enquire about them, but he never answered. She did not feel she should bother his mother, Naomi, yet.

Early in the war Eleanor had instituted a reassuring habit, as a calming effect, of meeting the two girls on their way home from school. At Lansdale Bridge they turned down the steps to walk along the River Thames. As they walked along the towpath that June, it suddenly seemed to be quiet and empty. It was then they realized that all the boats usually tied to wooden jetties along the banks had gone, even the smallest ones.

"How strange," Eleanor said, "they were all here only a few days ago."

Farther along the river they met a woman walking back and forth on the path. She told them that her husband had left three days ago in his small outboard motorboat. An urgent call had gone out to all boat owners with seaworthy craft to go across the English Channel and bring back British troops stranded in France. Every man she knew along the river had answered the call. Each day she patrolled the riverbank waiting for sight of any returning boats, but none had come. Eleanor and the girls quickly went home to pack a thermos of hot tea and sandwiches, then returned to join their new friend on her vigil. They sat on the bank with their legs dangling over the water and waited. As it began to turn dark, they heard engines coming up the river and, peering into the dusk, they saw the boats coming home, hundreds of them. A united effort had saved 338,000 servicemen, when it had been thought that, at best, only 20,000 to 30,000 could be brought home. Mr. Churchill called Dunkirk "a miracle of deliverance."

For the next two or three days Gwen and Jenny detoured past the railway crossing on their way to and from school. They watched the trains go by, loaded with soldiers from Dunkirk. As the trains sped through the crossing, the troops threw out letters and the girls and their friends quickly ran down the banks and onto the tracks to pick them up, putting them safely in their school satchels to take home. Eleanor stamped and mailed the letters, and this was how many families learned that their husbands, fathers, or sons were safely back on British soil.

Up until now Gowden Chemicals had escaped damage, but one night a twenty-five-pound bomb exploded on the roof, doing surprisingly little damage. Inexplicably, however, all the windows on the inner sides of a nearby three-story building surrounding a courtyard were sucked out. Rather than replace the glass, which could be blown out again, the administration decided to board up the windows, causing another problem—lack of light for workers in that part of the factory. But with need for medicines escalating, the government increased Gowden's electrical allowance so that future work could be done with the lights on all day.

During the repairs, Philip started going to work earlier than usual to check on the workmen's progress, which he felt was slower than necessary.

"You're not getting enough sleep," Eleanor grumbled. "You're up patrolling the streets three nights a week, and you barely get any sleep those nights, and on the other days you leave home by seven A.M."

"Well, what else can I do?" Philip answered, unusually edgy. "We've got to get back to full production again as soon as possible."

One of those early mornings, when Philip was walking to work, he ran into Colonel Adams out with his dog.

"Good morning, Colonel, it's good to see you."

Colonel Adams turned to him with stricken eyes.

Philip remembered how envious he had been as he watched the colonel parading with his regiment in the park just before they left for France. It wasn't even a year ago, Philip thought. Of the 1,000 local men so proudly parading that day, 700 had been killed in their first assault on the enemy. When ordered to take his remaining 300 soldiers back into battle, Colonel Adams had refused, and had been stripped of his command. He was a broken man.

On June 17, Philip drove to work. It was unusual these days, but he wanted to bring his longtime secretary, Miss Mott, home with him to listen to the prime minister speak on the wireless. The street was unusually quiet, and Philip knew that his neighbors, just like his own family, were waiting for the BBC broadcast to begin. Eleanor had cups of tea and biscuits ready for them.

In his short speech, Churchill told them that France had capitulated. This brought the Germans to within twenty-one miles of England's shores. They all sat in stunned silence, then Jenny burst into tears. The three other members of her family, and Miss Mott, all turned to look at her disapprovingly. They were in silent agreement that such weakness was not to be tolerated. Each new disaster must be met with stoicism.

Sensing their disapproval, and trying to control her sobs, Jenny said, "I can't help it. It's so terrible…I thought the French were our friends. What are we going to do?"

Eleanor leaned over, taking Jenny's hand in hers, "We can't give in to our fears now, darling. We've got to continue to be strong."

This was the first time Jenny had broken down. Indeed, neither

Gwen nor Jenny had shown any extreme emotion about the war. It was amazing that despite the daily upheaval in their lives, they seemed happy both in school and at home.

This school year, which was to end in mid-July, Jenny was lucky to have Miss Flora Atkins as her teacher, considered by parents to be one of the most conscientious in the school. Miss Atkins, an only and late child, had been cosseted by her doting parents during a lonely childhood. Now in her late twenties, she was belatedly enjoying the companionship of children by teaching a new class of twenty-eight twelve-year-olds each year.

Since the war began, Miss Atkins had weathered the sudden school evacuations to the air raid shelters whenever the sirens sounded. Shelters had been quickly built on school grounds and at other strategic places for the general public to use. Bus drivers had orders to stop at the closest one as soon as a siren went off. Each shelter had three bare electric lightbulbs spaced down its length, but most had no indoor plumbing; the "toilets" were buckets behind a sack curtain. Everyone tried to avoid the embarrassment of using them by holding out as long as possible.

Miss Atkins tried as best she could to gather her class close to her, huddling together on the long wooden benches stretching either side of the underground dugouts. Cold dampness oozed down the walls, which never dried out in the wet English climate. Miss Atkins then proceeded calmly to continue teaching her children their lessons, in seeming competition with two other teachers at either end of the same shelter, all trying to carry on and do the same thing.

It became more difficult when the Germans sent over a plane every hour, as a nuisance tactic, so that the air raid alarms were on all day and the underground shelters with eighty children and three teachers became chaotic prisons, but Miss Atkin regarded this as only an extra challenge. She stayed there after the school day was over, until early evening, when parents ventured out to take their children home, for she could not allow them to leave until the all-clear sounded.

The Battle of Britain began in June 1940. Then things changed for Miss Atkins, and she began to dread going to school. The terror started each morning as she tried to eat her bread and margarine and drink her tea with a sick feeling in the pit of her stomach. "How can I go on?" she wondered.

When Miss Atkins arrived at school, she usually went straight to her classroom. Now, sometimes when she hurried by the principal's office, the school secretary called out to her.

"Miss Atkins, Mrs. Hosford would like to see you."

"Oh dear," Miss Atkins answered, immediately alarmed. "Has there been…?"

"Yes," the secretary replied, looking distressed. "Just go right in, she's waiting for you."

Mrs. Hosford turned away from her desk to look at Miss Atkins as she entered. "My dear," she said sadly. "I'm sorry to have to tell you, there's been another one—Betty Sample, last night." Seeing the anguish on her young teacher's face, she quickly added, "Sit down for a few minutes, Flora, so you can collect yourself." Mrs. Hosford knew how hard it was for all her teachers, and for herself too. This was the sixth student to be killed in the last month.

Taking the school attendance at the beginning of the day was the duty that Miss Atkins came to fear most, especially after a night of heavy bombing. She began:

"Barbara Appleby?"

"Here."

"Jenny Bartlett?"

"Here."

"Patty Danby?"

"Here."

"Mary Elder?"

Silence.

Miss Atkins forced herself to look up, and before she could repeat the name, a child spoke up quietly. "She was killed last night with her mother and sister, but they got her father and her brother out, and they're in hospital."

"Thank you, Deidre, that's terrible news," Miss Atkins said, bowing her head. It was all she could do not to burst into tears, but she felt she had to set an example.

She looked out at the stoic, seemingly unfeeling faces of the students before her. She could never tell how they felt, for none of them ever showed emotion.

"I'm so sorry. We will remember them always," Miss Atkins said, then quickly began the day's lesson.

Sometimes students were absent because of family tragedies. Joan Thomas's father, an air raid warden, was killed one night, and Rosa Isley did not come to school after her brother was killed in action.

Despite knowing her students as well as she did, Miss Atkins had not understood their apparent imperviousness to the sadness surrounding them.

As soon as Jenny reached home, she cried as she told her mother about the loss of her school friend Mary Elder, who always sat next to her in class. She begged her mother to stop at the building and say a prayer for her the next day. Eleanor promised she would detour on the way to shop for food. She was amazed that the rescue squad had been able to get anyone out alive. The block of flats had collapsed like a deck of cards. Why hadn't they gone to the shelter, Eleanor wondered? Perhaps the children had been sick; but she also knew how hard it must be to take them out at night in the cold. She sighed before hurrying on her way. She was late, and the queue that always started even before the butcher and grocery shops opened would already be long. She worried that she would miss out on getting the food she needed for her family. Even amidst death, survival was always the most urgent instinct.

Queuing for food had become a part of daily life. It was a necessary nuisance, preventing people from doing something else they preferred. It was tiring to stand for so long as shopkeepers carefully cut out each customer's coupons, and it was uncomfortable, especially on hot and cold days.

There was an unspoken code of honor among those who queued, and woe to anyone who tried to break it. When the war started, it was sometimes difficult for those who had previously been more fortunate in life to accept that there was no way to avoid taking turns. Once Eleanor was standing in line when a famous actor's wife imperiously swept passed the queue and, walking straight up to the counter at the bakery, announced loudly, "I am Mrs. David Ortello!" The person cutting bread at the counter did not look up, but said quietly, "Yes, dear, but you'll have to take your place at the back of the queue like everyone else."

But Eleanor had to acknowledge that queues also served another purpose. There was a camaraderie among those who stood in line. No one got more than another unless supplies ran out; each one got the equivalent of one lamb chop per person per week as a meat ration, two ounces of bacon, and the same ration of all other basics. It was also a place for exchanging how-to tips, gossip, and other important information. Someone always knew which town "got it" in the previous night's bombing, before the newspapers printed it.

This is how Eleanor learned of the Critchley bombing from a sad aunt of one of the children. She and Philip remembered the village well, for they had often taken the long bus trip there on Sundays for tea when they were newly married. It used to be a charming and happy place. German bomber planes often flew beyond their targets because the barrage balloons afloat over London prevented them from getting down low. To lighten their loads before turning for home, they jettisoned their bombs anywhere they could. Lansdale, just west of London, sometimes received these bombs. But the enemy plane that reached Critchley, a village deep in the country, was far off course. The bomb could have fallen in a field, causing little damage. Instead it landed on the school, killing every child and teacher in it. Each family in the village lost someone.

One morning, in assembly after school prayers, Mrs. Hosford announced, "Tomorrow afternoon Mr. Churchill will be coming to Lansdale Green, and school will close early so you can go to see him." The students were thrilled.

Eleanor joined them and the large crowd that gathered to greet Mr. and Mrs. Churchill. They had begun to squeeze such excursions into their busy schedules, perhaps to keep up morale while London was enduring fifty-three consecutive nights of bombing. The Churchills were driven around the green in an open car, and when it stopped Mr. Churchill stood up to make one of his stirring speeches. Someone in the crowd shouted, "We can take it, Winnie, just keep on giving it to 'em back!" and the crowd roared in support.

As soon as Churchill began to speak, Eleanor felt her spirits lift from the gloom that had overtaken her during all those nights of constant bombing. His speeches always affected her this way. They were very powerful and inspired her to have hope again. "If I feel like this at my age," she thought to herself, "the young and impressionable must feel it even more strongly." She looked over at Jenny, who always carried her emotions closer to the surface than either she or Gwen, and she seemed transfixed. Jenny believed Churchill's words with a fervor and committed to memory those parts which affected her most:

"We shall defend every village, every town and every city. We should rather see London laid in ruins...than it should be enslaved.... London will be fought street by street. We shall defend our island whatever the cost may be. We shall fight on the beaches...on the landing grounds...and in the fields and in the streets and in the hills. We shall never surrender. Every man and woman, therefore, prepare himself to do his duty. This is the time to stand together. Hitler has kindled a fire in the British heart."

Jenny repeated these words often to herself as she lay on her cot in the cellar at night, listening to the bombs falling and the British guns responding in defense. The noise from both was deafening.

Jenny knew that she would answer Mr. Churchill's call and join with others to take up whatever weapons they had (in her case, only a carving knife). She imagined that they would fight, never giving up, until the last of them was backed into the Irish Sea. Jenny also sensed a sure knowledge that she would survive. But she did not feel that same assurance about her family. Coming home from school after a day of sudden bombing, she would peer around the corner where her home was to see if it was still there. Jenny knew that without her family she would be lost. It was her greatest fear. Although the war was everywhere, knowing that her parents and Gwen loved her gave her the illusory feeling of safety.

• • •

"Mrs. Hosford told us at prayers this morning that Miss Atkins is taking a leave of absence," Gwen reported.

"Oh, really?" Eleanor was surprised. "I wonder why?"

"Well, her mother died a few months ago, and now her father isn't well."

"I'm so sorry. I hope she'll come back to school soon."

"The girls in her class say she's having a nervous breakdown," Jenny volunteered. "She keeps on telling them to be quiet or else she'll scream."

"That's terrible," Eleanor said, "and so unlike her. She was always so calm."

"Mr. Boxley will be sorry," Jenny said.

"Mr. Boxley?" Eleanor asked, perplexed. He was the school's art teacher. He hadn't been called up because he had a limp.

"Yes," Jenny answered. "He really likes her."

Eleanor couldn't see that the two of them would be at all congenial. Mr. Boxley had always struck her as being very "arty" and quite bohemian in his lifestyle, whereas Miss Atkins appeared old-fashioned, even prim.

The girls were always full of news, and a week later Jenny came home with some more.

"Barbara Appleby's going to America," she said. "She's in my class and the only girl in the school who's accepted the invitation."

America and Canada had offered to receive evacuated British children to protect them from the bombing, and people over there were already generously offering to take children into their homes.

It was a kind gesture, the Bartletts agreed, but they would not even consider it.

"The Atlantic is far too dangerous," Philip said. "It could be even worse on the high seas than here. Do you remember Mrs. Dawnton?"

Mrs. Dawnton had lived in Lansdale in a large house with a beautiful garden going down to the river. For some reason she had been even more afraid of bombs than anyone else. Her husband, a wealthy industrialist, had tried to comfort her by tearing up the large lawn and building a completely reinforced apartment underground. Yet she had still been petrified, and eventually decided to go by ship to New York. Enroute across the ocean her ship had been torpedoed, and all passengers and crew lost. Meantime, her beautiful home and garden remained unscathed.

Barbara Appleby, however, arrived safely in New York and lived happily in Connecticut.

Chapter 10

"WE HAVEN'T SEEN YOU for so long," Peggy Edmonds said. "I haven't got enough to give you lunch, but can you come for bridge and tea on Saturday? We all need some fun. These constant air raids are frazzling everyone's nerves."

"We'd love to come," Eleanor replied quickly. "I agree, we do need a change from these nightly poundings. Poor Philip has been spending so many nights out on the streets as a warden. And we haven't been getting much sleep, either, with all those noisy anti-aircraft guns at the corner of the street."

The guns, which rolled silently out of the dark each night, were a mystery. And they were gone before daylight. No one knew where they were hidden during the day. It was thought that they were camouflaged and stored in the spinneys of Lansdale Park. But of one thing all were sure: what goes up must come down, and the neighborhood was convinced that British guns were causing much of the shrapnel damage to their roofs and windows.

"Then we'll see you as soon after lunch as you can make it," Peggy said. "Charlie bought the boys a new Charlie Chaplin or Buster Keaton film, I can't remember which, so they'll want to run it for the girls on their movie projector."

As the Bartletts drove from Lansdale to Upper Newton, a south-eastern suburb of London just an hour away, Eleanor said, "Jack will be eighteen on September 15, and he's signed up for the RAF."

"So this'll be the last time we see him before he goes," Philip replied. "Thanks for reminding me." It was already September 7.

The Edmondses' three-story house was set back from the road, with a circular driveway and two gates. It was a very nice area in which to live, and the gardens both front and back were spacious and well tended.

"This big house can't be kept up well with only a twice-weekly char," Peggy said.

"It looks lovely, as usual," Eleanor replied tactfully, but she agreed that it was a very large house.

The four parents settled down to their bridge game promptly, and Charlie dealt.

Peggy continued to grumble. "Did you see that disgraceful garden across the road? It's been bought by two buskers, and they stand at the bus stop every afternoon at 4:00 P.M., he with his accordion and she with her banjo, to go to London to entertain the theater queues. Then they come home on the last bus at 11:00 P.M. and sleep all day. So low class," she added, forgetting that she had come from a similar family herself.

"They must make a lot of money to buy a house like that," Philip said, astounded.

"Oh, they do," Charlie answered, "and since it's all cash, I bet they don't pay taxes on it. They must've got the house for a good price, though, because values have dropped around here since the war began. These houses are really too large to run without a lot of help." This comment, regrettably, started Peggy off on her grumbles again.

In the den, Jack set up the equipment to show the Charlie Chaplin film. After he had run it through once, Billy asked, "Can I do it now? I want to show him running up and down the hill." He got to this part and then reversed and had Charlie running down the hill backwards. He repeated this twice, going faster and faster, until the film snapped.

"Now you've done it," Jack said, all upset. "Dad'll be mad 'cause he just bought it. Why do you always have to spoil things?"

"Why am I always blamed for everything?" Billy asked unreasonably.

Gwen and Jenny sat there without saying anything. They were used to these arguments. They had known Billy for nine years, ever since he was five, and they knew him well. His exceedingly good looks were matched by his terrible temper, and he was prone to get into trouble. They both remembered one November 5, Guy Fawkes Night, when a firework had not started spinning properly and Billy had lost his temper after giving it a nudge and singeing his eyebrow off. The girls began to laugh at him again now, but before he could turn on them the siren sounded.

"That's strange," Jack said. "We haven't had a day raid for ages." The four parents came in.

"We'd better go down to the shelter," Charlie said.

"All of you take a couple of plates of food with you, and we'll have tea down there," Peggy ordered.

Gunfire started immediately, and Jenny ran as fast as she could, balancing two plates of sandwiches. She glanced upward, and the sky seemed to be covered with ants; but they were planes, fighters and bombers battling up there against each other.

The shelter was well equipped with crockery and a kettle and lots of games to play. The two families continued their games and had tea. Even through the heavy door they could hear loud gunfire. Suddenly they were shaken by a big explosion, and a lamp, hanging on the wall, fell off and broke.

"That was a close one," Charlie said. When things quieted down, he opened the door from time to time to see if the dog-fight above was still going on, and after a while they heard the all-clear.

Philip was anxious to get home, so they started off immediately. As they retraced their steps across South London, everything seemed calm and quiet, as though nothing had happened. They were relieved to find no damage to their house. As day turned into evening, they saw a red glow in the sky towards London.

"Let's go into the park for a clearer view," Philip suggested. When they got there, it seemed to them that the whole of London was on fire. But they learned from a park ranger that it was East London, the Docklands, that had taken such a beating, with 448 civilians killed and many more wounded.

Bombs had also been dropped that day in other parts of southern England. As the family walked back down the hill from the park and turned on Crescent Hill, they saw a policeman lean his bicycle outside their gate and walk up to the front door.

"Anything wrong, officer?" Philip called out.

"Well, yes sir. Could I have a word with you?" The two men spoke together outside while the others went into the house. Eleanor anxiously glanced out the window every few minutes until Philip came in.

"What's wrong?" she asked. "Something at the office?"

"No, it's Dad…he was killed today."

"Oh, I'm so sorry darling," and she went over to kiss him. "How did it happen?"

"He was sitting in the pub, enjoying his last glass of beer, when a bomb hit and killed them all. He'd gone with his pals to celebrate his birthday today," Philip sounded sad but bemused. "I bet he was spending the check I sent him. If it had to happen, though, he'd have chosen it this way."

"Poor old soul, he certainly was one of a kind," Eleanor said. She had often been annoyed with him, especially over the last few years, when he had gotten into the habit of asking Philip for "loans" with increasing frequency so that he could continue to enjoy his life to the fullest. Frederick Bartlett had succeeded until age seventy-nine.

Two weeks later, Peggy, weeping, phoned Eleanor. "Jack's gone. He left this morning, and I'm heartbroken."

"I know, and I'm sorry," Eleanor said, sympathetically.

"He wants to be a fighter pilot, and it's so dangerous."

"I doubt if they'll let him because of his eyes," Eleanor answered, practical as usual. Jack had always worn glasses.

"You know, Peggy," she continued, "I've been thinking. You really need a project."

"A project!" Peggy exploded. "How can I fit any more in, with this big house to look after and queueing and everything."

"Close off the top floor, and make Billy keep his own room and bathroom clean and tidy. Then you only have your own bedroom and bathroom to look after, and the char can keep the ground floor spic and span, and sometimes even go to the shops for you."

"Charlie's pretty fussy about the house."

"Everyone's got to give a little, even Charlie," Eleanor continued. "Do volunteer work; I just love my Red Cross knitting group, and we have a lot of laughs. I always feel very cheerful when I leave. Or, another idea, Charlie's always complaining about staffing problems. Why don't you go back to work in one of his shops?"

"I don't think he'd like that," Peggy said slowly, "but I'll think about what you said. I know you're only trying to help," she added grudgingly.

Then, later in the month, Philip got a phone call at the office.

"I say, old chap," Charlie said. "Could you and Eleanor come over this evening after work? Peggy isn't well."

"Yes, I think so," Philip answered, wondering if he had enough petrol. "What's wrong with her?"

"We'll explain it when you come," Charlie said quickly. "Thanks so much," and he hung up.

"It's all very mysterious," Philip said, when he phoned to tell Eleanor. "But I promised we'd go."

They left the girls at home with their neighbors, Mr. and Mrs. Rose, and as soon as they arrived, Charlie ushered them upstairs. Peggy was in bed, looking miserable.

"Let's go downstairs and have a drink," Charlie suggested to Philip, leaving the two women alone.

"What's the matter?" Eleanor asked.

"Well, I got pregnant and I tried to fix it, and I think I've got an infection."

"What does the doctor say?"

"I haven't been to one."

"What did you do?" Eleanor asked, and when Peggy told her, she was horrified. "A crochet needle, how could you, Peggy? It's so dangerous."

"I know, but I was desperate. Nothing else worked. I thought you'd be able to help me."

"It's been nearly twenty years since I was a nurse, and even then

I only tended men with war wounds. I wouldn't know what to do."

Peggy began to cry. "I feel such a fool," she sobbed. "Charlie has always played around, and I've always known, but I shut my eyes to it because I was determined not to let him go. So when he wants me, I always agree. This time I most probably had a little too much to drink, and I was careless."

"Let's call your doctor now," Eleanor begged, but Peggy was reluctant.

"No, but I've got the name of a local gynecologist I've heard about."

Eleanor phoned him, explained the situation, and was quick to state her own lack of involvement. He agreed to come immediately. When he arrived, Eleanor met him at the front door, looking him over as she took him upstairs. "Dr. Gardner seems pretty urbane to me," she thought, "I bet this isn't the first time he's been called out to deal with such a problem."

There was something about him she didn't like. His black hair was slicked back with Brilliantine, and he had an ingratiating and smooth manner. She was sure he'd submit an especially hefty bill, charging a fee according to the ability of the patient to pay.

Eleanor was waiting for him on the landing when he came out of the bedroom.

"I've given her an internal medicine, cleaned her out, and treated the wound with an antiseptic. I'm pretty sure we caught it in time, but you were right to call me. I'll come around tomorrow to check on her again."

When Eleanor went in to see Peggy, she already sounded better, almost perky.

"What a nice man," she said brightly. "When I'm healed, I'm going to have a procedure done so this won't ever happen again."

Charlie was relieved that the problem, to his mind, had been so easily solved. He made light of the matter to Philip, but the Bartletts always took life more seriously than either of the Edmondses.

As Philip drove home, Eleanor filled him in with the details, adding thoughtfully: "When people die or have their lives ruined by war, we grieve terribly. So it's upsetting when people treat life so carelessly and with no thought of any consequence. And Peggy could have died, too."

"Perhaps you find that thought the most disturbing of all," Philip said gently, putting his hand over hers. "You've really become very fond of her."

"I know," and Eleanor smiled. "Despite all her grumblings over the years, I've grown to love her."

Chapter 11

JANET MARSHALL SOUNDED unusually excited when she phoned.

"Can you come to lunch on Saturday?" she asked. "Patrick O'Shea is passing through London, and when he called wanting to see us, I impulsively invited him to lunch." Janet had always enjoyed the O'Shea family; perhaps she saw in them a mirror of herself, with their lack of adornments.

"I thought you might like to see him too," she continued. "I haven't got much to feed all of you, except an abundance of vegetables and fruit we put up last summer. Bring the girls, too. The boys always enjoy seeing them."

"We'd love to come." Eleanor was enthusiastic, for these were the short, depressing days of winter. "I'll try to get some fish to bring."

"That would be lovely, dear, if you can. Then we can all have a dab of it."

Janet met them at the door when they arrived.

"Patrick's already here, and you'll be surprised. He's joined the army as a chaplain." And there he was, as huge as ever and very handsome in his uniform.

The only member of his Dutch family in England, young Willem Jonkeer was also there, having been evacuated with British troops at Dunkirk. He was now a corporal, stationed with a small contingent of Dutch soldiers in a London barracks. He had not heard a word from his family in Holland. Willem came to the Marshall home often in hopes of seeing Christine, but she seldom seemed to come home.

There was never a suggestion of serving drinks before meals at the Marshall home, so Janet said, "Let's sit down to lunch and we can visit as we eat." The maid, ever-faithful Alice, had already started serving.

"Janet, you're an absolute wonder," Eleanor exclaimed, admiring the colorful table. "I've never known anyone as clever as you to make food look so delicious and go so far. It really looks like a feast."

"It's mainly vegetables," replied Janet modestly, but with justifiable pride.

"Is that cauliflower au gratin?" Philip asked, peering at the table. "I hope you didn't use up the family's cheese ration on it." Everyone laughed as they sat down to enjoy it, plus potato and spinach salads, a dab of Eleanor's fish, and the inevitable sausages. Sausages were a mainstay on the British war time diet, and the butt of many jokes. It was said that "the meat just walked by the sausages," for they were mainly stuffed with bread, and no matter how many times they were pricked with a fork, they still expanded when fried and burst all over the frying pan.

"Tell us the news of your family, Patrick," Peter Marshall said.

"I've just seen Mary and Maureen in St. Anne's to say goodbye," Patrick began. "Kathleen is still in St. Albans, and I saw her last night. She's still working there and waiting for Terence, whenever he can get leave."

"And your mother, Eileen, and Kevin, how are they?"

"Mam complains of her legs," Patrick continued, "but I hope that isn't serious; Eileen is fine, and Kevin is really enjoying his work in the diocese of Cork. It seems to be the perfect niche for him. He's much more interested in the inner workings of the church than in parish work, and I'm the exact opposite."

"How's the communication system working with Ireland?" Philip asked.

"It's working pretty well. We all write and send letters in a packet to Boston, cousin Daniel mails it to Ireland, and we get letters that way too. The other good news is that Daniel's Boston parish is a large and wealthy one, and they raise a lot of money for the poor in Ireland. He's added Mam's name to the list to receive her share of it. It's a great help to her and a relief to us. We never asked him to do it, but it's wonderful."

Over pudding of apple crumble, Philip turned to Willem, remembering amidst all this family talk that he was cut off from his own family in Holland.

"Have you seen your Aunt Naomi recently?"

"Not for a while," Willem replied, adding candidly, "She's not very well, really, and sometimes I feel she doesn't remember who I am. She only wants to talk about Valerie, Paul, and my mother." They were all silent for a minute, for this is what they had feared.

"Perhaps you see Paul?" Eleanor suggested.

"No, I think he's traveling around the world to trouble spots for the Foreign Office. He shares a flat with his boss, Michael Wisley, but he never seems to be home," Willem replied.

Eleanor already suspected this, since she could never reach him either.

"How's Christine?" Patrick asked, turning to Peter.

"She's stationed in Portsmouth," her father answered. "She seems to be working very hard in the WRENS, but she doesn't get much leave, so we don't see her often. Do you ever see her?" he asked Willem, who perked up considerably.

"As often as I can," he said.

Eleanor had never been close to Christine. Indeed, she had disapproved of the freedom that her parents allowed Christine during those holidays at Whitney Bay, so she was taken aback when she answered the phone in April and a young girl's voice asked, "Mrs. Bartlett?"

"Yes," Eleanor answered hesitantly.

"This is Christine Marshall."

"My dear, how nice to hear from you," Eleanor said, trying to hide her surprise.

"I'm going to be close by tomorrow morning, and I was wondering if I could stop by to see you?"

"Why don't you come for tea in the afternoon. The girls will be home from school then, and they'd love to see you too."

"I can't," Christine replied. "I have to catch the two-o'clock train back to Portsmouth." Eleanor felt a pang of annoyance. Tuesday was the day the grocery shop got its deliveries, so she had to go there in the morning, and she hated to feel rushed, as sometimes the queue moved so slowly.

"Well, why don't you come at eleven-o'clock," she suggested. "I'll go out to the shops as early as I can, and if I'm not home by then, I'll be sure to be home in a few minutes. Then we can sit down and have a good visit."

She arrived home a few minutes early and was putting the groceries away when the doorbell rang. Christine looked pale and thin. "War weary," Eleanor thought, "just like the rest of us." Portsmouth had been taking the brunt of a lot of bombing lately.

"It's lovely to see you, Christine," Eleanor said, pouring tea for the two of them. "I'm so sorry Portsmouth has been getting such a beating. I'm sure it's been terrible."

"No worse than anywhere else, I expect," Christine answered, looking down at her hands. Then she blurted out, "I hope you don't mind my coming to see you, Mrs. Bartlett."

"Of course not, dear," Eleanor murmured, waiting.

"I'm going to have a baby, and I don't know what to do." Eleanor immediately thought of Willem Jonkeer.

"Perhaps if you told the father, he might want to marry you," she suggested.

"Oh no, when I told him, he said he was already married and had two children, which I didn't know about, and that I'd have to handle the problem myself. And I really loved him too," Christine added, tears rolling down her cheeks.

"I'm so sorry, dear," Eleanor said, leaning over and holding her hand.

"I need to have an abortion, but I don't know who to go to. I tried to find someone who does them last night, but when I got to the address I'd been given, the building had been bombed."

Eleanor momentarily thought of Dr. Gardner, then immediately dismissed the idea, shocked at herself for thinking of him. He was such an oily character, and his practice was too close to Peter Marshall's anyway. Eleanor was sure that even if their paths had not already crossed, Peter would know his reputation from the medical grapevine, and he would disapprove of him. So she just said, "I don't know of anyone at all, but the very best people to turn to are your parents."

"Oh, I couldn't go to them," Christine interrupted, even more agitated. "They've never understood me at all."

"But they love you so," Eleanor persevered, "and I know they'd help you to come to the right decision."

"Willem said that too."

"Oh, he knows?"

"Yes, I met him and told him last night. He said he'd marry me, if that's what I wanted."

Eleanor was appalled to think that these two nineteen-year-olds would even think of getting married for all the wrong reasons.

"Do you love him?" she asked.

"No," Christine said truthfully, "but he loves me."

"I think it would be terribly hard to be married to someone you didn't love," Eleanor said slowly. "I really want to help you, dear, but I don't know how to. I could make some enquiries tomorrow, but I can't say if she'll be able to help. How can I reach you in Portsmouth?" The person she would ask, Eleanor quickly decided, was Mrs. Derby, her charwoman, who was much more worldly about such matters than she.

"Thank you, but I feel I have to make a decision now," Christine said miserably, getting up to leave. They kissed, and Eleanor watched her walk along the path and out the gate, feeling that she had failed her.

As she passed the hall mirror, Eleanor peered at her image. "This is the second time in a few months that I've been approached on this same subject," she said to herself, "and I hope there won't be a third."

Two weeks later, Janet Marshall phoned.

"I've got some surprising but exciting news," she said. "Christine called yesterday to tell us that she and Willem got married. Of course, we wish they had waited so that we could have had a lovely garden wedding, but they said they had to do it when their leaves coincided."

Eleanor was silent for a moment, then gathered her wits to sound enthusiastic.

"That's lovely news. Willem is such a nice boy, and I do hope they'll be very happy. Will they be coming home soon?"

"We hope so. Yes, I do agree that Willem is a wonderful boy, and I feel he'll be good for Christine, maybe calm her down a bit. They've certainly known each other a long time, and even though they're so young I find it a comfort that it wasn't a fly-by-night marriage. I must go," Janet added. "This is my day for helping out at Peter's office."

As December 1941 arrived, there was reason for more hope: the USA declared war, and Christine Marshall Jonkeer gave birth to a little boy—the first grandchild to be born to a Whitney Bay family.

When Janet phoned to tell them, she said, "They're calling him Pieter. It's half English, half Dutch. He's healthy, though small, almost six pounds, but then he was early. Willem is getting leave so he can come to see his new little son."

Eleanor immediately sent off the baby cardigan she had started to knit as soon as she heard that Christine had married Willem. She made it of yellow tweed wool, suitable for a boy or a girl, and in a one-year size. She considered it impractical to knit anything smaller, since babies grow so quickly in their early months. Because she didn't want to fall behind in her Red Cross knitting, she chose to stay up later each evening to knit the little sweater until it was finished.

Eleanor still regretted not being able to help Christine when she asked. She thought about the young couple and the step they had taken. Christine was now back home where she didn't want to be. But perhaps now, with a baby, she would be less restless. No matter what, she and the baby would be well cared for by her parents. Eleanor found herself worrying more about Willem, still only nineteen and alone in England with no family to advise him.

Chapter 12

AS SOON AS SHE HEARD Peggy's voice on the phone, Eleanor realized that they had not spoken for some time.

"I've done what you suggested," Peggy said briskly.

"What was that?"

"I've gone back to work."

"Are you enjoying it?"

"Well, it was quite difficult at first." As usual, Peggy was slow to admit that she enjoyed something. "But actually I am."

"What are you doing?"

"I'm working for Charlie again, as head of personnel for the greater London area. I go around hiring—we never fire anyone anymore, since we can't get enough help. I also run training sessions for new employees." She sounded so enthusiastic.

When they hung up, Eleanor felt a pang of envy. It would be exciting to be working again, she thought. She could go back to nursing to help the war effort. But then it wouldn't be fair to the girls, and she needed to watch over them even more now that they were growing up and demanding more freedom. Although Eleanor never learned to drive, swim, or play tennis, she wanted her girls to experience the things that she had been too timid to try. But now she was fearful for their safety from bombs—and from men. Britain, a tiny island, had been invaded not by the enemy, but by allies. The country was already full of men, and since the arrival of the US troops it seemed overwhelmed. Worldly wise from her experience as a World War I army nurse, Eleanor allowed that most men were well behaved, but she argued with herself that when men were far from home, they had little accounting to do about their behavior. So she became more watchful, and from stories she heard, her fears were not unfounded.

Philip tried to act as an intermediary between the girls and their mother, and he was sometimes able to persuade Eleanor to let them go to the cinema. Once, while there, a bomb dropped nearby without warning. Gwen and Jenny, hearing glass breaking and seeing plaster falling, clung to each other and stayed in their seats, fearful that they would be crushed by many in the audience who were panicking and running for the exits. They did not dare to mention this to their mother for fear that she would never let them go to the cinema again. Indeed, they didn't tell their mother a lot of things now.

All their young girlfriends became streetwise in handling each new situation, and they shared these experiences with each other. They were shrewd in their evaluations of men who approached them, and invented a rating system by country, starting with the worst: Poles, French Canadians, free French, Americans, Australians, New Zealanders, Canadians, and British (who, of course, had families closer at hand).

Gwen was always the drawing card, for she was tall, slender, and very pretty. Jenny was the extra dividend. Even when they were in school uniform and the men knew they were young, it made no difference. Their apparent creed was, "If they're big enough they're old enough." The US servicemen, especially, tried to bribe them with promises of steak and ice cream if the girls would meet them the next day.

Peggy, however, had no such worries. Her older son, Jack, had been given a ground job in the RAF in central England, and Billy Edmonds was still too young to join up. He did not seem to miss Jack at all. He enjoyed being the only one at home, and he found it a relief not to have Jack constantly ordering him around or looking over his shoulder to prevent him from getting into trouble.

Billy spent a lot of time mooning over the Bartlett girls. His mother was realistic enough to suspect that neither of them would have him; they knew him too well. Also, Billy once foolishly told Jenny that he could not decide which one of them he preferred, weighing the quieter and more elegant Gwen against Jenny, who might be more fun. This was a major mistake because the two sisters never poached on each other's territory, especially where boys were concerned. This problem did not occur when airman Jim Marshall (neither of the Marshall's two older children had been persuaded by their parents to become conscientious objectors) developed a strong, though silent, affection for Gwen. It could never have been Jenny, for she was far too lively for him.

Having a job made Peggy more efficient. She always did a quick dusting before she left in the morning, was first in the queue at the shops on the days her char did not come, and was gone before ten-thirty by car or train.

One Friday morning she took the train to Victoria Station, then took a taxi to Bond Street to interview applicants for one of their upscale "Madame" group of shops. After that session, she had a quick lunch and tried to get a taxi to Marble Arch, where she was to interview again for their more modest "Marietta" group. All the taxis were full, so she finally decided to walk via a shortcut on the back streets.

Peggy always dressed especially well for interviews and training sessions, in order to emphasize to the new saleswomen that if they were hoping to sell lovely clothes, they had to look smart themselves. It was a difficult pitch with wartime clothing coupons. She was wearing her new black suit and high heels, and when she looked in the mirror before she left home, she assured herself she looked good, perhaps even sensational.

Soon after she started walking, Peggy regretted the high heels. She turned the corner into a side street to find a rope barrier across it. "Damn," she said to herself, "now I'll have to take a detour, and my feet are really hurting." Then she peered ahead, and through the smoke and dust she saw the collapsed building.

"When did this happen?" she asked a demolition worker.

"At four this morning. A direct hit."

"Well, at least these are offices and shops," Peggy said, "so no one was in there at that early hour."

"There were tenement flats on top, and we've been hearing the people in there scream all morning begging us to get them out." The man sounded angry and tired. "But move along, miss, you can't stay here."

Peggy wasn't planning to stay at this scene of desolation. The air was acrid from the explosion, and she could now hear the muffled cries of people still buried in the building. A pipe twisted and bent twelve feet up, cracked under the weight of the fallen bricks and a brown liquid dripped out, making rivulets in the dust on the ground below.

As she started to leave, she glanced once more at the piles of rubble. Something caught her eye, and she leaned farther over the barrier to look at it. There, just above the ground, amidst the layers of collapsed floors and ceilings, she saw something sticking out, and it moved.

"Oh, my God! There's a hand sticking out there! I saw it move." And she bent under the rope and ran forward, stumbling across the broken pieces of building which lay all over. "It's a woman's hand," she cried.

"You can't go in there, it's dangerous," the man called agitatedly, but Peggy took no notice. She knelt and took hold of the hand, asking, "Can you hear me?"

She heard a moan, and a faint voice, "My Gawd, you 'eard me. I've been screaming all morning. I'm 'urt awful bad. It's me legs."

A policeman came along. "You'll have to move along, madam," he said severely, but Peggy wasn't listening.

"Now, we've found you," she said to the woman, "I'll stay with you till they get you out." She looked at the policeman and sat down.

"You can't stay here," he said again, and in a lower voice, "and they're not going to be able to get them out."

"Oh, no…then please, let me stay with her," Peggy pleaded.

"It's against orders, madam," he said, looking around nervously, "but all right, just for a few minutes."

Peggy continued to hold the woman's hand. It was rough and careworn, with short and broken nails.

"Are they clearing the bricks on top of me?"

"Yes," Peggy lied.

"I live on the fourth floor...there's only two floors above me...it shouldn't take long."

"No," Peggy said. "Did anyone else live with you?"

"Not now," the woman said, "me 'ubby's at sea...been gawn six months...and me boys evacuated to somewhere in the middle of England...can't remember the name."

"How old are they?"

"Eight and ten." Then the voice added, "It's a sauce."

"A sauce!" Peggy repeated, astounded, and then she thought quickly, tomato, hollandaise, bernaise, H.P., Worcester.

"Worcester?" she asked.

"S'right...the address says 'near Worcester'...can't remember the village." Then she cried out loud, "Me legs 'urt something awful, one of me 'ands is stuck down here, and it's sticky."

"What's your name?" Peggy asked gently.

"Violet 'Enry."

"Do you work, Violet?"

"I'm a waitress at Lyons Tea Shop...'Yde Park Corner." The voice was growing weaker. Violet did not talk anymore, but she continued to squeeze Peggy's hand in response.

The sun sunk behind the buildings that remained standing on the west side of the street and it was getting colder, but Peggy stayed on. The policeman handed her a cup of tea when he walked by, but he pretended he did not know she was there.

The cries for help were fewer now, and an eerie quiet descended as demolition workers were sent off to other sites across London where they could be of more use.

Sitting there, Peggy tried to visualize Violet's life, living alone, her husband and sons gone; working on her feet all day and coming home at night to a cold and shabby tenement flat. It must have been a life without comforts. Thoughts which Peggy had kept hidden for a long time, even from herself, now crowded into her mind and forced her to recognize what she had become. She had been determined to forget her own humble beginnings in her haste to enjoy everything Charlie's money could buy. Peggy now realized what a selfish and greedy person she had become.

Violet was not answering her squeeze any more. Peggy lifted up her hand and let it go; it fell into her lap. She got up stiffly and slowly retraced her steps to the Bond Street shop. It had already closed. A taxi stopped to let out a passenger.

"Can you take me home to Upper Newton?" Peggy asked the driver. "I'll pay you extra."

"It's an awful long way, miss," he replied, and then he looked at her. "But I can see you've 'ad a bad day; 'op in, luv." Peggy cried all the way home.

Charlie came out of the house as soon as the taxi turned into the driveway.

"Where've you been? I phoned the shops, and nobody knew anything, I've been so worried." And then he looked at her. He'd never seen her in such a state—her new suit covered in dust, stockings torn, shoes scratched, and big streaks on her face. He paid the taxi driver and took her in his arms. Peggy continued to cry.

"Why don't you take a quick bath and climb into bed?" he said. "And then I'll bring you up a stiff drink."

Peggy stayed in bed all weekend. She told Charlie a little, but didn't seem able to talk about what was bothering her. When he asked her what was wrong, she'd just cry and say, "This bloody war, that's what."

"I've never seen her like this before," Charlie told Philip, whom he always phoned when things were not going well. "She's usually so spunky; I can't imagine what's got into her. It's not like this is the first time she's seen the devastation of war, although it's the closest she's been to it."

"Do you want Eleanor to call her?"

"Yes, I think that'd be a good idea."

But Eleanor refused. "I'm not going to bother her. I know Peggy very well, and she likes to work things out for herself first. She'll call me, I know, when she's good and ready." Peggy phoned five days later.

"I'm sorry you had such a nasty experience, Peg," Eleanor began.

"Yes, it was terrible," Peggy answered. "I've never been with a dying person before, but I was glad to be there with her. That isn't what hit me, though. As I was sitting there holding that poor woman's hand, I really thought about myself. And I was ashamed."

"Why?" Eleanor asked.

"You of all people should know why; you've often had to listen to all my petty grumblings."

"You weren't that bad," Eleanor said, laughing.

"Yes, I was. From my own low beginnings, not much better than poor Violet's, I've become a selfish and greedy snob. Some of it may've been because of Charlie's chasing women, but I knew he did that when I married him. The funny thing is, I know he loves me. Do you think there's any hope for me to change?"

"Oh, yes," Eleanor said affectionately. "Lots."

"Another thing," Peggy continued, "I want to track down those two Henry boys. I've already talked to the people at Lyons, and they think they're in the village of Upshaw, just outside Worcester. Your cousin, Mary Wilson, doesn't live far from there. Perhaps she would help me find them."

"I'm sure she will. I'll write her."

Mary began immediately to do some detective work, but she couldn't find the boys through her vicar. Apparently, they were not churchgoers. A week later, however, she went to her evacuation hosts' group meeting, where people discussed their problems with the children they housed. There Mary met a Mrs. Janet Ennicott, who had come to discuss her evacuees, Arthur and Tom Henry.

Peggy was relieved to get the boys' address, and she immediately sat down to write them that night after work. Mrs. Ennicott reported that both boys had been brave when they heard the sad news about their mother. She also wrote that they were well, often mischievous, and that the younger boy, Tom, told her that he was glad his mum had had a kind lady with her when she died.

Peggy continued to write them, sending Mrs. Ennicott money to buy clothes for the boys, always enclosing some extra pocket money for treats.

Chapter 13

IN THE SUMMER OF 1942, Gwen was to become eighteen. She sat for her finals in school, which she was leaving at the end of the term in mid-July. It was a time of stress because on her birthday in August she had to register for national service, stating a preference for a wartime occupation; otherwise she would arbitrarily be assigned to any service which had an urgent need at the time.

The family was fearful, worrying with Gwen over her decision. She just couldn't make up her mind, so it seemed easier to make the choice by a process of elimination.

Philip started off. "Would you like to be a landgirl?" he asked. But before Gwen could answer, Eleanor dismissed the idea.

"No, she can't do that, she's not strong enough. Farming is hard physical work, and she'd have to be up at 4:00 A.M. milking cows, carting hay to feed the animals, or driving a tractor. It's far too heavy work."

They methodically continued down the list. Working in a factory was also eliminated. Gwen then considered the three women's services in the army, navy, and air force, but she couldn't work up any enthusiasm for them either.

Jenny was encouraging. "You'd look awfully good in the blue air force uniform, Gwen," she said.

"What about working in a government office? You might be

lucky enough to get a job in London, so you could live at home," Eleanor suggested hopefully. But Gwen answered decisively, "No, I'd be put in a typing pool, and all the girls I know just hate it."

Finally Philip asked her, "Is there anything you'd particularly like to do, dear?"

"I just can't see myself working only with things—sending up barrage balloons, making weapons, driving a tractor, or typing letters," Gwen said in her usual sweet manner. "I'd like to have more personal contact with people, so I think I'll be a nurse, like Mummy." Eleanor was surprised; she'd never noticed any burning desire in Gwen to become a nurse, as she had felt when she was young, but secretly she was pleased.

Just as in the First World War, a call went out for qualified nurses, and the government needed to train them as quickly as possible. But only conscripts with the highest marks from their schools' advanced exams would qualify, so the family nervously waited to hear Gwen's results. They were good; she was top of her class.

"I always knew you could do it," Jenny said admiringly. "You've got all the brains in the family."

Within two weeks, Gwen left for nursing college outside Norwich. The family missed her terribly. It was the first time they had ever been separated for any length of time.

As parents, Philip and Eleanor never worried about Gwen. She was always a good student, whereas Jenny, at best, was a disinterested one, and at worst a lazy one. All her report cards said, "Jenny could do better," and her teachers often asked her, "Why can't you be more like Gwen?" After each report card, Philip would give Jenny a talking to, but it never seemed to do any good.

She became even more dissatisfied with school, enviously imagining that now Gwen could do anything she wanted. She made herself unhappier by dwelling on all the things she missed. It was mainly food. No one had seen a banana, an orange, a grapefruit, or a lemon since the war began. The fruit had to be imported; cargo ships bringing food into Britain were confined to carrying only essential supplies, and often they were torpedoed en route. Jenny began to complain that she was often hungry (though never starving), since the overly starchy food did not fill for very long.

Eleanor was doing her best to feed the three of them left at home. She sorely missed Gwen's ration book, which had gone with her to Norwich, for these extra rations allowed for a little more variety of menu. She was also growing weary of Jenny's complaints.

"All you young people get extra milk," Eleanor said impatiently. "Think of poor Mr. and Mrs. Rose down the road, who only get a half-pint of milk a day for the two of them. And the national bread we get uses the whole kernel, so it's healthier." She did not mention that it soured quickly because it had no preservatives, nor did she remind Jenny that for years she had given the girls her own one egg that she got every six weeks. Still vivid in her memory was seeing a woman cry when the egg she so carefully placed on top of her groceries in her canvas bag toppled out and broke on the pavement. All the women nearby sympathized with her in her mourning.

"We're all weary of war and miss having a lot of things," Eleanor continued, gathering momentum, "but there's nothing we can do about it, so there's no use in grumbling. I'm glad we can give our babies orange concentrate, cod-liver oil, and vitamins. I've never seen a more healthy lot sitting up in their prams with their rosy cheeks."

Jenny thought better than to start complaining about the lack of glamor in their clothes. She hated the opaque, beige, lisle-cotton stockings that they had to wear. She felt they made her legs look thick, and they were so worn they were virtually darning hole to hole.

The only women who now wore nylon stockings in England were US servicewomen, or the prostitutes on the street she saw when she went up to London to meet her great-aunt Jane for tea. They were the best-dressed women in town. As Jenny and her maiden aunt sat drinking tea in a small tea shop off Regent Street, they both looked out with interest at the women parading up and down the street. Their solicitation was very discreet, and the men were polite. One elderly man even doffed his hat, and Jenny imagined him saying, "No, thank you, dear, not today."

"He's most probably flattered to be asked," Aunt Jane sniffed.

Eleanor was disturbed by Jenny's litany of complaints; it was unlike her, for she was usually happy and positive. Eleanor knew she missed Gwen, but 1942 had also been a difficult year for the Allies. There had been many setbacks which affected people's morale, and this might be one of the causes of Jenny's problems, she thought.

On September 8, an attempt to invade France at Dieppe was made and quickly repulsed by the Germans.

"I'm not surprised," Philip said to Eleanor in exasperation. "If you heard in the queue last week that it was going to happen, then I'm sure the Germans heard it too and were lying in wait for us to arrive." Eleanor agreed. A woman had told her that her daughter's French Canadian boyfriend had mentioned that the British and Canadians were going to invade France at Dieppe. At the time, she considered it idle gossip, nevertheless she repeated it to Philip.

"We'll have to do better than that next time," Philip said. "If we're going to broadcast our plans, we'll never win."

The war in North Africa had not been going well either. This worried Eleanor because her nephew, Dylan, was fighting over there, and Terence Murphy, Kathleen O'Shea's husband, was also in Africa.

But in November there was cause for celebration, because the Allies had won a tremendous victory at El Alamein. As the Bartletts walked to church the following Sunday, Eleanor stopped.

"Listen! Can you hear the bells?" And suddenly bells were pealing all over the Thames Valley.

"They're beautiful," Jenny said, remembering the joyful sound from years ago.

"I never realized how much I missed them," Eleanor continued. "I always loved hearing them when I was a child in Wales, walking across the fields to church, especially in the snow."

Church bells had been silenced at the beginning of the war, to be used only if the country was invaded. The government waited one more year before allowing the bells to be rung every Sunday, thus giving everyone hope that the threat of invasion was over.

• • •

When Jenny told her parents that she didn't want to continue at Lansdale School for Girls, they were taken aback, for she was only sixteen.

"We hoped you would stay on until you were eighteen, just like Gwen did. You did so well in your general schools exams, too," Philip protested.

But Jenny had laid her plans well. A year earlier, she had finally started to work harder in school, had really studied for these exams, and had received four honors. She was bored with all the petty regimentations of the school which she had attended since kindergarten. She wanted to move on.

"I don't want to waste my time staying on in school," she insisted. "I want to work and replace someone who has had to go away to war. I know I can be useful."

Jenny looked over at Gwen, who was home for the weekend. But Gwen said nothing. If her parents asked her, she would side with Jenny. She always did, because she admired her younger sister for fighting for what she wanted.

Philip sighed, "We'll think about it, dear. You'll have to be trained to do something."

The compromise her parents came up with was a one-year course at a secretarial college in London. Jenny immediately accepted.

In September, Jenny started her courses at St. Martin's College for Gentlewomen. At first glance, it did not seem that she had succeeded in changing her way of life, but going up to London every day gave her a feeling of freedom. St. Martin's was just across the road from Buckingham Palace, and often Jenny climbed to the top floor to see if anyone was walking in the garden. She knew the royal family had chosen to stay in London during the Blitz, but she never saw anyone.

A mix of young women from all over Britain came to St. Martin's. Many were older than Jenny—daughters of farmers, industrialists, politicians, middle-class, and aristocrats. Some were war widows who needed to renew their secretarial skills in order to go out to work again. Most of the students lived in London, sharing apartments; but some, like Jenny, traveled back and forth daily to their homes in the suburbs.

Philip and Eleanor felt they had chosen well. They had heard of St. Martin's good reputation from many friends. Its director, the Honorable Miss Fiona Ellison (referred to by her students as "The Hon") was the daughter of a lord, and all the other teachers were her social, as well as her business, friends. One of the most popular courses at the college was the acted-out "How to Handle Men and Stop Their Advances." Jenny later learned (and certainly her parents did not know) that most of the women connected with the college were lesbians.

A month after the term started, two of her new friends told Jenny that they had found good volunteer jobs, and they urged her to work with them serving food in the evening to servicemen at Australia House. Jenny had never worked before, except to pack food boxes for the poor at church or wrap knitted garments for the troops, but it sounded like fun. The job was only three stops beyond Victoria Station, where she got off daily, so she could still use the Underground season ticket her father had given her without dipping into her small weekly allowance for the fare. Already Jenny had an innate interest in handling money well.

At the interview with the manager of the canteen, the rules were laid out:

1. Hours 6:00 to 9:00 P.M., two nights weekly.
2. Duties: prepare food, serve it, and clean up after.
3. There would be an experienced supervisor on duty.
4. Volunteers were to be pleasant and friendly, but there was to be no fraternization on the job.
5. Supper would be provided.

These last magic words were the clincher. Jenny knew that her mother would be relieved not to have to give her supper two nights a week. She was to work Tuesdays and Thursdays.

Jenny began her job the following week. Margaret Merton was her supervisor both nights. A pert little twenty-six-year-old blond,

Margaret had worked in the canteen since it opened in 1940. She could be strict when she thought things were getting out of hand, but she was always fair. Many of the volunteers were older single women of about thirty, mostly government workers in nearby Whitehall, but the nightly crew of eight got along well, often traveling partway home together as a group. When the Underground train stopped at each station, they saw the population of London preparing for bed on the station benches or cement floor. This is where they came to sleep safely, away from the nightly Blitz. Jenny wondered how they could sleep with trains passing through every few minutes until after midnight, and was thankful for her cot in the privacy of the basement of her own home.

The men who came to the canteen were well behaved, looking for a cheap night out in London where they could get a meal and meet people from their hometowns. If they wanted more excitement, they could go to the pubs or dancehalls. Sometimes, one of them would hand over a large bag of canned fruit, and the crew that night divided it up and took it home. No one asked where it came from, or whether it had been stolen from an army kitchen. And nothing was asked in return.

The men were served just tea and real coffee, not the "ersatz" coffee sold in the shops, which tasted and smelled like rubber. The menu always included one hot dish with vegetables, sandwiches, cakes, and, the most delicious of all, waffles with ice cream and strawberry sauce. None of the volunteers had eaten waffles before.

One night, after the girls arrived, they were ushered into the back pantry. A doctor came in to tell them that a contingent of wounded men were coming in. They were airmen, he explained, whose planes had crashed in flames or into burning oil tanks in Italy. Their burns had healed, and they had come to London for plastic surgery.

"I want to emphasize," he continued, "how important it is for their morale that you not change expression when you see them. We have to heal their minds as well as their bodies." The volunteers all quickly agreed that they would smile and joke as usual.

"But it was so hard," Jenny said, crying to her beloved Gwen, who had just arrived home for a thirty-six-hour leave. "How horrible and painful it must have been for them. I kept on talking and smiling, but they didn't have any faces, just blobs with four holes in them."

During the two years of their treatment, the burned men returned to the canteen regularly, at first in groups and then individually as they regained confidence. The girls applauded as the men proudly showed off their new noses, cheeks, chins, and eyelids. And at the end, Jenny could not believe that such miracles had been accomplished to make them look normal again.

The men joked, "I'm more handsome now than I ever was. My family won't recognize me when I go home."

One of them, Joe Stillman, came in more often than the others. He became quite a fixture and often helped to clear up before they closed at nine o'clock.

When the usual group went home together on the Tube, one of them commented that she thought Margaret Merton and Joe Stillman were a couple.

"Oh," Jenny said. "I never thought of it, but perhaps you're right. He does always stay until after we leave. Anyway, Margaret seems to have fooled us all by strictly honoring the 'no fraternization on the job' rule."

Chapter 14

EACH CHRISTMAS CAME and went with less joy and celebration as the war continued, but still messages were exchanged.

In 1943, Ena Thompson wrote from the Earlwood Boys' School:

> Our elderly headmaster, Mr. Harrison, retired in June, and Ralph took over as headmaster of the school. We are both working so hard to keep everything on an even keel here. So many of the boys go straight off to war as soon as they finish school.

There was joyful news from the O'Shea family. Mary wrote:

> Kathleen had a little girl, Erin, on September 14. Terence hasn't seen her yet, as he's still in Africa. This is Mam's first (and perhaps only) grandchild from all six of us. We hear no news from Ireland since America entered the war.

There was a card, this time signed by Pashi, for Naomi Patterson with his usual note saying, "Madam and I often speak of those happy years we all spent together in Whitney Bay. She enjoys reminiscing."

Of course, there was no news from the Jonkeers in Holland. Janet Marshall always mentioned Willem Jonkeer when she phoned or wrote. Janet was now looking after her grandson, Pieter, while Christine, still living at home, worked full-time in her father's medical office. The grandparents were very contented with this arrangement, but Eleanor wondered if Christine felt the same way.

In preparing for the Normandy invasions, the USA, which had welcomed so many Irish to its shores, requested that Ireland close off its diplomatic relations with Germany, thus preventing Germany from spying in Ireland and their U-boats from refueling in Irish ports. But Eire refused.

America must have felt as the British did when they asked France, before it capitulated, to send to Britain their 400 prisoners of war. France promised to do so, but instead returned all of them to Germany, thereby ensuring that they would fight against Britain another time.

Late in spring of 1944, Jenny was invited for the weekend by her St. Martin's College friend, Sylvia Hunt. It was to celebrate the coming end of the school term, after which both of them would be starting jobs.

Sylvia's parents, Marcia and Paul Hunt, were giving another of their parties. Because they entertained constantly, they were also asked out a lot, and it made them feel better if their only child, Sylvia, felt free to invite her own friends home.

Paul, a leading government architect, used to travel to countries in the British Empire supervising additions to embassies and government buildings. He had enjoyed these trips and now he had to content himself by inviting servicemen from the countries he had previously visited to his own home. This weekend a group of US servicemen were coming for the first time, and Paul wanted to make the evening especially enjoyable.

"It'd be nice if you would play the piano, dear," Paul said to his wife, "while the rest of us dance. I've got lots of drinks in."

Marcia's cousin, Anita, who lived nearby, had already arrived to help with preparations. She was always available for a party, especially when her husband was at sea in the navy. A few other couples from the neighborhood were also coming.

"And then there are the two girls. By the way, where are they?" Paul asked.

"They've gone for a bike ride, but they should be home by now. Where've you been?" Marcia demanded when they walked in the door. "Better go upstairs to change. The guests will be arriving about seven."

Lieutenant Harrison Sanders came to the party with three army friends, all lieutenants. He had been born twenty-seven years ago in New York, but now lived in California, where his mother's family came from. After graduating from college, he had gone on to law school and worked in San Francisco for a year before joining the army. He had tried to enlist when Pearl Harbor was bombed, but had been turned down because of his eyes. However, he had kept on trying and had finally been accepted by the Signal Intelligence Service.

Harry noticed Jenny as soon as he arrived and asked her to dance when Marcia sat down to play. His friend, Jack Tenby, from New York, made a beeline for Sylvia. They could not dance together all evening, as everyone changed partners frequently, but Harry asked Jenny for her telephone number before she left. Jack Tenby asked Sylvia for hers too. One of the Americans, the Texan, walked Anita home.

The two girls talked about the party before they went to sleep. Sylvia really liked Jack. After Sylvia fell asleep, Jenny felt strangely wide awake.

When Harry phoned two days later, Eleanor answered and was immediately on her guard. She sounded fearful yet forbidding, and Harry quickly understood that she did not like, or, as a protective mother, was frightened of American soldiers. He then spoke to Jenny and felt better when she agreed to meet him for dinner.

This anti-American reaction, however, did not deter Harry from calling again, although he always prayed that it would not be Eleanor who answered the phone. He knew that his time in

England might be limited, and his main desire was to see Jenny. He did not expect to be invited to her home, realizing from his initial conversation with her mother that he would not be welcome. And it did not occur to either Philip or Eleanor to invite him because they considered this friendship to be only a passing one.

Jenny soon began her first job at a women's magazine on Fleet Street, and Harry was relieved that he could phone her at the office. Theirs was an uncomplicated relationship, going out to dinner or a film and enjoying being together. Sylvia's friendship with Jack Tenby, on the other hand, blossomed early into a passionate, even torrid, affair, but after a few months it abated and died a natural death.

After Harry went to France, Jenny felt the loss more than when all her other friends went off to war. It was always sad to say good-bye. But he continued to write, and she always answered his letters promptly.

Billy Edmonds had also left recently to join the army. His mother was more resigned to his leaving home and did not appear to be as upset as when Jack had gone earlier in the war. Billy asked Jenny to see him off. He might have asked Gwen if she had been around. Both girls often went to the station when boys asked, more out of friendship than romantic inclination. The boys wanted to be seen with a girl waving them off.

When Christmas came in 1944, there was no news from the Thompsons, no news from the O'Sheas, and no card from Naomi Patterson's Pashi.

"Oh, dear," Eleanor said to Philip. "I fear they have forgotten us."

"I'll bet they haven't," Philip answered soothingly. "People are so busy nowadays, I'm sure you'll hear soon."

Eleanor checked with the Edmondses and Marshalls, but they hadn't heard anything either.

Mary O'Shea was the first to write in the new year:

We had no spirit in us to celebrate Christmas this year.

Terence was killed in North Africa in early December. He never saw his baby, now sixteen months old. We have moved Kathleen and baby Erin to St. Anne's to be with us. Patrick brought her up when she moved. It was such a comfort to be together. There's no contact with Ireland, but we wouldn't have the heart to tell them this sad news anyway.

The following month, Eleanor read of Ralph Thompson's death in the paper. In reply to Eleanor's sympathy letter, Ena wrote:

Ralph worked so hard as headmaster of Earlwood School, and he could not slow down as the doctor ordered. He had a massive heart attack on December 10. He rallied well, and we thought he was recovering, but he had another one in February. We had been married for thirty years, and I don't feel whole without him.

To lose two old friends so close together was such a blow. Eleanor considered Ralph's death war related too, as he had taken on so much extra work because of the shortage of help. When she opened the paper two weeks later and saw two more obituaries, it was almost more than she could bear. She phoned Philip at work, something she never did, and he came right home. He picked up the paper to read:

JONKEER, killed by a bomb near Amsterdam, Holland. Margot Marlow Jonkeer, her husband, Jan, and four of their five children, Till, Sybil, Ingrid, and Tania.

Then farther down in the same column:

PATTERSON, Paul, beloved son of Mrs. Naomi Patterson, killed on war duty. Aged thirty-five.

"That's strange," Philip said. "Neither of them said when."

"Poor, poor Naomi, now she's lost everyone," Eleanor said

tearfully. Then she remembered Willem, the only Jonkeer left, now a member of the Marshall family. "Perhaps it's good after all that Willem married Christine. Oh, I do hope so," and she wept again.

When she recovered, they discussed what they should do.

"I think you should phone Naomi," Philip said. "You can always follow up with a letter. I sense that it happened some time ago, so the sooner you contact them the better."

Eleanor was uncertain whether this was the best thing to do, but she dialed the number. It rang and rang. Finally, just as she was going to hang up, Pashi answered.

"Pashi," Eleanor said, "it's all too terrible, but I felt I had to talk to you. How can Mrs. Patterson bear any more tragedies?"

"Ah, Mrs. Bartlett, how kind of you to call," Pashi said, always so proper. "Yes, Madam is completely inconsolable."

"It seems particularly sad that they should all die so close together in time," Eleanor continued, feeling that perhaps she should not have said that, in case he thought she was probing.

"I do not know all the facts, Mrs. Bartlett, other than Mr. Paul worked for the Foreign Office, and sometimes that involved danger."

"Is there anything we can do for Mrs. Patterson?"

"You have always been such a good friend." Pashi sounded so sad, and Eleanor realized that this was just as much a loss for him, since the Pattersons had become his family too. "But there is really nothing that can help her. She is not well and lives very much in the past these days, which is really better for her."

"Please tell her I phoned and that I will write her."

"Thank you for your kindness. I certainly will tell Madam you called. We talk of you so often. I know she will remember you," Pashi said before he hung up.

Both Philip and Eleanor agreed that there was something strange about all this.

"How could it be known in England about a bombing in Holland?" Philip queried. "Communication is broken between the two countries. Do you think they heard about it through the Foreign Office?"

"I don't know, but I'm so thankful that Naomi has Pashi," Eleanor said. "She just couldn't get along without him." This was something Pashi thought about more and more, for he was now sixty-five years old and he feared that, should he die first, Naomi would be completely lost.

When the conversation with Eleanor ended, Pashi reflected for a moment before going to tell Naomi about the phone call. He went over with her once again their reminiscences of those many years ago.

Soon after they had received the shocking news about both the Jonkeer family and Paul, Michael Wisley, Paul's longtime boss at the Foreign Office, drove from London to Naomi's home in Buckinghamshire to give his condolences.

He felt a heavy responsibility for this tragic conclusion to his request to Margot Jonkeer that halcyon day on the beach at Whitney Bay in 1939. He wondered whether it had been necessary, and anguished over the answer. To have lost a whole family, with four children and Paul too, affected him deeply. It was also a terrible personal loss, for Paul was not only his best friend, they had been lovers too.

Michael knew that he could not allow personal feelings to interfere with his professional decisions. He tried to argue with himself that in his position of overseeing all security and intelligence for his country, his duty was to weigh losses against gains when exposing his staff and others to danger. He knew that in this particular case, the gains had been overwhelming. In addition to allowing twelve British agents to use their home many times as a haven and message center for exchanges of critical information, nineteen escaped British prisoners of war had also passed through the Jonkeer home on their way to safety.

As soon as he arrived, Michael was appalled by Naomi's decline in health, mind, and appearance. He quickly realized that Pashi was in complete charge, and so it was to him he addressed his remarks. Pashi listened impassively, for he continued to conduct himself in the role of servant.

"I feel I should tell you some of the details of this tragedy,"

Michael began, "but for security reasons, it must be kept in strictest confidence. I know you understand this." Pashi nodded.

"Mr. Paul was a British agent for the Foreign Office for many years," Michael continued. "We needed to have our own spies strategically placed among our allies on the continent in order to gain important intelligence for us. When Holland, Belgium, and France fell, Paul remained over there. Sometimes he needed a place to hide where he knew he could be safe. It must have been this need which took him to the Jonkeer's home outside Amsterdam. I know he would have been exceedingly careful not to place the family in danger. We think a local person was bribed by the Germans to inform on them, and they then blew up the house, killing them all."

"Are you going to tell this to Mr. Willem?"

"No," Michael said. "I don't want to yet."

Michael felt he had explained the situation sufficiently. He did not say how many people had used the secret room underneath the house, because this might reveal why the "safe house" had become an "unsafe house."

Pashi listened to the explanation in his usual impervious manner. He found it difficult to grasp that Paul, whom he had known and loved since he was a little boy, could have become such a fearless man. Deep down in his heart, Pashi had often regarded Paul as a rather weak and effete person, and now he regretted and felt shame for having had such thoughts and for having been so wrong. This knowledge added to his complete dejection as he looked lovingly across the room at the person who had once been the radiant and beautiful Naomi Marlow Patterson.

Chapter 15

THE ROUTINE OF LIFE continued, amazingly similar to that of peacetime, with a variety of discordant disasters woven in. Eleanor found comfort in doing the same things she had always done, especially when she was sad. She did not, however, include going to the dentist in this category, but she had chipped her front tooth on a hard slice of toast at breakfast and felt it should be taken care of before any more broke off. Luckily, the dentist could fit her in that afternoon.

A sign on the inner door of the waiting room said, "Ring bell to let nurse know you are her." Eleanor rang, and a nurse appeared, saying, "Take a seat, Mrs. Bartlett."

A man came in and repeated the procedure. Eleanor glanced at him. He was a short, overweight man approaching fifty, with a florid complexion. He smiled at her. Sensing that he might want to start up a conversation, Eleanor got up and crossed the room to pick up a copy of *The Lady* from the table alongside the wall. She returned to her chair and started flipping the pages of the magazine, but soon realized that it must be prewar, with so many pictures of luscious food. She looked at the date; it was over five years old.

Suddenly she tensed. Was that a buzz bomb coming this way? She listened intently and noticed that the man also appeared to be listening. The sound came closer, and Eleanor hoped that this manless machine would continue to pass over them. Until the engine stopped and it started to come down, a buzz bomb was not dangerous. But no one knew what direction it had taken until it exploded.

They heard the engine stop, and both Eleanor and the man quickly and noisily scrambled under the table. It was a tight squeeze, perhaps tighter than necessary, Eleanor thought, and she moved away from the man as far as she could. She could tell that he'd had a beer or two with his lunch.

"This is ridiculous," she said to him after a minute had passed. He smiled at her again, and unconsciously she moved her knees closer together.

"Nice weather today," the man said.

"Yes," Eleanor replied, politely.

"But it may rain later," he added.

"Oh," Eleanor said.

The minutes ticked by. "It must've gone off by now," Eleanor said. "It usually only takes two or three minutes."

"I didn't hear it," the man answered.

The door opened, and the nurse came out. Seeing the empty chairs, she called out, "Mrs. Bartlett?" and then she saw the two of them still under the table.

"Oh, there you are!"

"Did the bomb go off?" Eleanor asked, immediately getting up.

"Yes, very quickly, and quite far away."

The man crawled out, brushing himself off. "That must've been when we were rushing to get under the table," he said laughing, and added, "Anyway, we had a good time."

The nurse turned to look at her questioningly as Eleanor, visibly annoyed, followed her into the dentist.

Eleanor decided to go home via High Street to see if there were any bakery goods left. She was not very hopeful at this late hour.

As she turned the corner, she almost collided with a woman pushing a pram.

"Mrs. Bartlett!" the woman said.

Eleanor looked at her more closely. "Why, it's Miss Atkins!" she exclaimed, remembering the young teacher who had left the girls' school. Then she looked at the baby.

"It's Mrs. Boxley now," the woman answered shyly.

"Oh, how nice! And is this your dear little girl?" Eleanor said kindly, restraining herself from leaning forward to wipe the baby's nose, which was dribbling down her upper lip.

"Yes, this is Mary Anne," her mother answered proudly, apparently oblivious of the runny nose.

"How old is she?"

"She was three in April."

"I'm sure you're too busy to go back to teaching now!"

"Yes, and my parents left me the house, so we're just able to manage."

"Glad to know you're doing so well," Eleanor said as she left.

Miss Atkins has changed so much, Eleanor thought to herself; she used to be so neatly dressed, and now she looked quite bedraggled. She must have taken on Mr. Boxley's ways, with his unkempt hair, sandals, and arty clothes. And they must have married very soon after she left school if the baby was already three, Eleanor decided as she hurried on.

Just as she had feared, nothing was left on display in the bakery shop window, but she decided to go inside anyway.

"Are there any buns left?" Eleanor asked.

"No, they're all gone, dear," the baker's wife replied. "But you're in luck. My hubby said today that he was so tired of just making bread, he decided to make tarts with some strawberry jam he was saving for a cake. I can let you have three."

"Oh! What a treat! We'll have them for supper."

Eleanor could not have been more pleased as she carefully carried the tarts home in the fragile paper bag.

The V-1 buzz bomb raids were soon replaced by V-2 rocket bombs. It was generally agreed that Hitler, fearing that he was now losing ground to the Allies, was determined to frighten and exhaust the British by creating all these atrocities to rain down on them, and yet the British never lost their spirit to fight on.

Each week, Eleanor looked forward to Wednesday. It was the day she went to the Red Cross meeting. She always stopped at the vicarage on the way, to pick up her friend, Margaret Rogers, the vicar's wife. Together they walked, chatting all the way, through the vicarage garden gate, across the churchyard, and on to the parish hall.

Margaret and Eleanor had been good friends for over twenty years, ever since the Bartletts moved to Lansdale just after they were married. Church had been the pinnacle of Eleanor's social life as a child in North Wales, and it continued to be an important part of her life now.

Sometimes Margaret asked Eleanor to attend a funeral or memorial service with her, especially when she felt it might not be well attended, or if there was a special need. She had done this the previous week, when the butcher's delivery boy, Tom Marker, had been blown to bits by a rocket bomb while cycling down Church Road. These rockets came so unexpectedly out of the sky that at first people thought the explosions were caused by bursting gas mains.

"Please do come on Saturday, Eleanor," Margaret begged. "We want as many people as possible, for the family's sake. They're devastated; he was only sixteen."

"Of course, I'll come," Eleanor replied. "I knew Tom well, and I feel so sad about it. He'd only been working there a few months, since he left school in July."

They went to the service together, the whole congregation grieving with the bereaved family. As they were leaving the church, Miss Larson, an old parishioner, limped up to them.

"Such a terrible thing," she murmured. "I was his final delivery, so I was the last person to see him alive. I wish he'd stopped to talk to me a few minutes longer, but he was always in such a hurry to get back to the shop. Will this war never end?" she added sadly as she shuffled off home.

About twenty women gathered for the meeting. They enjoyed visiting with each other as they knitted. Some of the women took extra khaki wool home with them to try to finish another pair of socks or a Balaclava helmet during the week. At first, Eleanor tried to encourage Gwen and Jenny to knit too, but they always ran into trouble with the sock heels and toes, which delayed her own progress when she had to set them straight. Finally, she just gave them the darning to do instead.

Mary Penfold, the Red Cross representative, was in charge of wrapping the weekly parcel of knitted clothing for the troops. Each week she persuaded everyone to donate whatever piece of wrapping paper and string they could spare. These things were scarce, and it was a sacrifice to give them away. Each woman also brought a teaspoon of tea leaves so they could enjoy cups of tea with their lunch.

Sometimes they were asked to stop knitting in order to make emergency blankets for babies in hospitals.

Most of the women were from Lansdale, but a few came by bus from neighboring towns. Fiona Martin was one of these, and when they stopped for lunch she was anxious to tell them her story.

"I had a bit of luck going to the bus after the meeting last week. I found a piece of liver on Church Road. It must've been dropped by a careless butcher's boy. It was all unwrapped, and I took it home in my scarf and washed it. We all had a piece of it for supper. It was a real treat, I can tell you." The other women marvelled at her good fortune. Eleanor shot a quick glance at Margaret; her face was impassive. They both remained silent.

As the two of them retraced their steps to the vicarage, and as soon as they were out of earshot, Margaret asked, "Well, what did you think of Fiona's story?"

"It's a terrible thought," Eleanor answered, "but Miss Larson did say that Tom was on his way back to the shop after making all of his deliveries," and she put her hands to her face and burst out laughing.

"Eleanor!" Margaret was shocked.

"I'm sorry," Eleanor said, trying to stop laughing. "But I just can't help it. It's so awful, we might as well laugh as cry." She laughed again and added, "And everyone was so envious."

"At last! At last!" the cry went out on V.E. Day, May 8, 1945. "The war in Europe has ended!"

Church bells rang out joyously, and the people of Britain, even those who had lost loved ones, felt that the future had changed from night to day. Everyone rejoiced with each other that now their men would come home, families would be together again, and they'd be able to buy anything they wanted.

On hearing the news, Gwen got the night off to go to London from Oxford with a group of other nurses and medical students from her hospital. They wanted to see the king and queen greet the crowd outside Buckingham Palace. She arranged to meet Jenny in front of old St. Martin's College, now a bombed-out shell.

The group made their way toward the palace, together with thousands of others. The crowd was already so enormous around the fountain that they could not see anything. Gwen declined to get up on the shoulders of one of the students to see what was going on, but Jenny was game to try it. As she was hoisted up and rose above the throng, she called out, "The crowd is huge and spreads for miles up the Mall and all over St. James's Park. Oh!" she added excitedly, "the king and queen are coming out onto the balcony, and so are the two princesses." A roar erupted from the crowd and the royal family stayed there a long time waving to them, but the crowd would not let them go. When they finally went back inside the palace, the crowd began to disperse; but nobody wanted to go home yet. Gwen and Jenny walked up the Mall with their friends, twenty abreast, arms around each other. The bells of St. Martin-in-the-Fields at Trafalgar Square were still pealing. They walked miles, down Whitehall, back along the Embankment, and up the Strand. When the rest of the group agreed they wanted to stay up all night to see the sunrise, Gwen and Jenny decided to go home and ran to catch the last train at midnight. Their parents, hearing them come in an hour later, were relieved.

It was a short night; Gwen had to be up early the next morning to catch the first train back to the hospital in time to work the day shift.

But for those in the Pacific, still fighting the Japanese, peace had not yet come. Another three months passed before World War II finally ended. When V.J. Day came, on August 15, the British celebrated all over again, but in a more subdued manner. It seemed that all their energies were spent. In the interim months they had learned that the scars of war were going to take longer to heal. It was to be another nine years, until 1954, before food rationing ended.

Harry's unit, Signal Intelligence Service, stayed on in Paris after the war ended to supply communications to US troops remaining in France. In late August he was moved to a camp near Lille, in northern France. This raised both Harry's and Jenny's hopes that he would return to England to embark for the US from Southhampton or Liverpool. But in September he wrote disappointedly that he was to leave for home directly from Cherbourg.

Jenny was philosophical. She had never wanted or expected to go to America to live, as many other British girls wanted to do; she had just thought that sometime, in the far distant future, she might enjoy a holiday there.

But by the next time Gwen came home, Jenny confided how bitterly disappointed she was. "I really wanted to see him again, to be sure I felt the same way, especially since I am so much older now." Gwen smiled and was as sympathetic as ever.

Nevertheless, the friendship not only survived the separation, it flourished.

Chapter 16

October, 1947

WHEN HARRISON AND JENNY Sanders left their wedding reception at Lansdale Town Hall, the guests followed them out into the street, loudly calling out their good-byes. The limousine took them to Victoria Station, and they went on by train into the country of Kent, called "the garden of England." Harry had often come down to some stables nearby to ride when he was stationed in London. But this time they were staying at an old Tudor inn, the Beacon, with a great collection of copper pans around the large open fireplace in the huge entry hall and famous in prewar days for its good food. When they arrived they were shown to their bedroom, charmingly furnished with antiques. The bed was a four-poster and the floor, with its handsome oriental rug, was gently sloping, not unusual in Tudor houses. In the corner of the room was a more modern touch, a hand basin with hot and cold running water. The bathroom was two doors down the hall.

On returning to their room after dinner, they found that a fire had already been lit. They undressed and lay on the thick rug in front of the fireplace and made love for the first time. They stayed there until the fire died down, then they moved to the bed and made love again before falling asleep.

The next morning upon waking, Jenny looked at her finger to

admire her newly acquired rings, and with a shock she saw that they were gone. Harry had had both the engagement and wedding rings specially made for her in San Francisco, and they were a little loose. She woke up Harry immediately, very upset, and he sprang out of bed to help her look. Jenny was more distressed at the loss of her wedding ring than her solitaire diamond ring.

"How can I go down to breakfast without my wedding ring?" she wailed. "I'd be too embarrassed." Harry tore off the sheets and blankets, and after shaking them all and finding nothing, they continued the search. Finally, on the ledge which supported the mattress and springs, they found the two rings.

Jenny, relieved and with unblemished reputation still intact, dressed and happily went down to breakfast.

For a week they enjoyed the good autumn weather and the peacefulness of the Kent countryside before leaving for Ostend and Brussels. Although it was only the beginning of November, there was a festive air, and already there were many signs of the approaching holiday season. They took side trips to Bruges, Antwerp, and Ghent before moving on to Paris.

When they arrived, a message from Aunt Edith was waiting at their hotel. She happened to be passing through Paris en route from visiting friends, and she invited them to dinner at Maxim's that night. Harry wanted to introduce Jenny to the opera, so he took her to *Carmen* at the Palais Garnier, and she took him to meet the Smythe family, who were as cordial as ever. Anabel even gave a party in their honor, inviting her many new young French friends.

It was a fancy honeymoon for a couple who, together, had very little money, and their travels had not ended yet. Still to come was crossing the Atlantic, a week or so in New York, and then the drive across the country to California via the southern route to avoid snow up north. They were to arrive in Cascade Valley by December 15.

Harry, usually careful with his money, wanted to use some of what he had saved from his army pay to stay longer on the continent alone with Jenny, for he realized that once they left England on the ship, they would have little time to themselves for the next two or three weeks. Soon enough, Harry reasoned, they would find themselves as poor as all the other young marrieds who were starting off after the war.

For the first few days after the wedding, Eleanor tried hard to adjust to Jenny's leaving. But she didn't have much time to dwell on it, for there were many "echoes" from friends who called to say what a lovely wedding it had been.

One of the first to call was Kathleen O'Shea, who had some cheering news. The four O'Shea sisters had bought a house in Lansdale. Eileen was moving from Ireland to live with them and already had a job. Mary and Maureen were continuing with their Board of Trade jobs, and the widowed Kathleen would run the house and stay home with her little girl, Erin.

"What a perfect arrangement!" Eleanor was thrilled. "It'll be wonderful to have you close by so Philip and I will have the pleasure of watching another little girl grow up. Kevin will miss Eileen, though," she added. "Do you think he'll come back to England now that you're all here?"

"No, I don't think so," Kathleen said quickly. "He's happy where he is and doing very well in the Cork diocese. Eileen didn't see him very much after Mam died, and we're delighted to have her here with us."

"And how is Patrick?" Eleanor asked. "I didn't have a moment to really talk to him at the wedding."

"Oh, he's fine. He stayed over to visit with us after the wedding." Kathleen hesitated. "I might as well tell you, as we've been friends for so long, he's leaving the priesthood. We were so shocked. I'm glad Mam isn't here, and I never thought I'd ever say that."

"What's he going to do?"

"He's going to run a settlement house for youth in the East End of London." Kathleen answered. "He's very enthusiastic about it, but we hope he's doing the right thing. He's always been very good with young people." Eleanor could tell that Kathleen was nervous.

Because the news about both her brothers was so recent,

Kathleen did not feel ready to share any more. Time enough, she thought, when we move to Lansdale.

What Eileen told them about Kevin distressed them all. Even before his mother died, Kevin had become deeply involved in Irish politics. Although he was a good and pious churchman, he had developed a deep hatred for the English, and this frightened them.

As for Patrick, the sisters didn't know what to think. In addition to his leaving the priesthood, he was going to marry an ex-nun he had met as a nurse in a hospital in France. The two of them were going to run the settlement house together.

"That was a beautiful wedding," Peggy Edmonds said enthusiastically when she phoned. "I bet it cost you a pretty penny, though." Eleanor laughed.

"Charlie and I both think Harry is a fine fellow, and so is his father," she added mischievously. Eleanor laughed again, for Peggy never missed noticing handsome men.

"I feel sure they'll be happy together," Peggy continued, knowing how sad Eleanor felt. "Harry certainly dotes on her, and they seem very well suited, so I know things will work out well for them."

"I do hope so," Eleanor said, then quickly changed the subject. "We were so happy that Naomi, Pashi, and Ena Thompson came. We never thought they would, but it wouldn't have been complete without them."

"Naomi's so frail and tottery, I'd never have recognized her if she hadn't been holding onto Pashi's arm," Peggy said. "And Ena, always so tiny, seems to have shrunk to nothing. Didn't Pashi look distinguished in his suit? He was quite the English gentleman."

"Yes, I don't think any of us ever saw him out of his white uniform." And then Eleanor added, "How was Whitney Bay?"

"Marvelous! Good weather, and we took the boys." With their own two boys grown and gone, when Peggy referred to "the boys," she meant Arthur and Tom Henry. "They always make us feel ten years younger."

As Peggy sat with their dying mother amidst the bomb rubble, she had vowed to herself that she'd watch out for Violet Henry's two boys, and this was a promise that she willingly kept. With their father still often away at sea, the boys moved in with their aunt when the war ended. Whenever Peggy visited one of their "Marietta" shops nearby, she always took them out to tea after school. Charlie was as enthusiastic as she was, and the two of them often took Arthur and Tom to a film, followed by a fish-and-chips supper.

When Charlie and Peggy opened their Whitney Bay house again, it seemed natural to take the Henry boys with them. By now, they all agreed, they were practically family.

The Marshalls were the only ones they hadn't heard from after the wedding. It was unlike them, and disturbing to Eleanor because they had always been such close friends. She feared she knew the reason.

Jim Marshall, one of the ushers and now a twenty-three-year-old medical student following in his father's footsteps, found a quiet moment at the wedding to talk to Gwen. He was fond of her, Gwen knew, but there had never been any overt signs whenever she went out with him to a film; he was very shy. So she was taken aback when he told her he loved her, asked her to wait for him to finish medical school, and said he wanted her to marry him then. Gwen loved him as a childhood friend; they had grown up together, but she found him too quiet, almost colorless. She needed someone more lively, and her thoughts turned to John Mitchell. Standing there, beautiful in her red velvet bridesmaid's gown, she quickly decided how to answer Jim. She wanted to be kind, but also truthful.

"You know I'm fond of you, Jim, but not in that way," Gwen began, and closed her eyes before she continued. "But I've met someone else, and if he asks me, I want to marry him." Jim looked stricken, and quickly walked away.

When she told her parents, they felt she had answered as best she could, but Eleanor continued to worry about not hearing from Janet.

"Most probably there's nothing wrong," Philip said. "Perhaps she's been extra busy with Pieter. Why don't you phone her? There's no point in your stewing about it."

Janet was guarded when Eleanor phoned, not her usual self at all. No mention was made of the wedding, and the conversation seemed stilted.

To break the ice, Eleanor asked, "How's young Pieter?"

"Wonderful, as usual."

"You'll miss him when he moves to Holland," Eleanor said. His father, Willem Jonkeer, had not come to the wedding because he was in Holland trying to start up his father's factory. "But you'll be able to visit them often," she added quickly.

"Pieter's not going." Janet's voice had an uncharacteristic sharpness to it. "Christine refuses to go; the marriage is over."

"I'm so sorry," Eleanor said, but Janet made no reply, and feeling the conversation was over, Eleanor added, "Please give my love to the family," before she hung up.

The four days Harry and Jenny spent in Lansdale were agony for Eleanor. She wished they had left for America directly from France, since their visit reopened her sense of impending loss all over again. They, on the other hand, thought it a kindness to return, hoping that the time away better prepared the family for their final departure.

But it was very hard to say good-bye. The two sisters cried together on that last night. Jenny knew she would miss Gwen more than anyone.

When the taxi arrived to take Harry and Jenny, with all their luggage, to Waterloo Station, Philip went out alone to see them off. After kissing Jenny good-bye, he shook hands with Harry.

"Please take good care of her," he said. "She's a good girl." And he turned quickly and went back into the house.

After taking the boat train to Southhampton, where the *Queen Mary* was berthed, they settled into their two-bedded cabin, and then went up on deck to watch the ship sail. But it was too windy and cold in the late November afternoon to stay there long, so they went into the large lounge filled with Americans, who were now, at last, free to travel to Europe. As the ship began to move out the orchestra played "God Save the King," and Jenny automatically stood up. She looked around her and discovered she stood alone. Leaving England was the moment she had dreaded just as much as leaving her family, but she willed herself not to cry in front of all those people. Harry quickly got up to stand beside her.

The first night at dinner, Dora announced to Jenny, "I've decided I want you to call me 'Mater.' It's so English, and I love Latin."

Jenny looked at Harry in amazement and replied nervously, "I don't think they've used that name in years, and then only among boys in public schools. I've never heard anyone call their mother, or their mother-in-law, Mater."

"It's the perfect name," Dora said firmly.

As soon as they got into their cabin, Jenny exploded. "I can't call her Mater. It's obsolete, and I'd feel so silly."

"That's fine with me," Harry said. "Why don't you call her 'Mother,' like I do." The matter was settled. Dora was disappointed, but after trying a few times to change their minds, she let it go.

The first two nights at sea, Dora took Jenny aside to sit with her after dinner, apart from the men, "So that father and son can have a nice visit together." Then she regaled Jenny with her thoughts on other matters. She had great admiration for her two daughters, Anna, a year older than Harry, and Grace, two years younger. "You could not meet two more intelligent girls," she said, then added quickly, "Of course, all my children are brilliant."

She would not allow herself any such admiration of her two sons-in-law, Anna's husband, Elton Millard, who lived near the Sanderses, and Grace's husband, Lee Sutley, in California. Indeed she expressed great disappointment in both. "I expected Grace, at least, to marry the president of Standard Oil," she complained.

"But are they happy?" Jenny ventured to ask.

"Oh, yes," Dora allowed grudgingly. "But I'm not."

Jenny later repeated all this to Harry. "I hope she's not going to be disappointed in me too. But I have a feeling that they were so relieved to have you marry at thirty that they'd accept me even if I was an elephant." Harry laughed out loud.

But fate stepped in to allow Jenny to forego these nightly chats.

The ship ran into stormy weather, and she discovered that she was not a good sailor. For the next three nights, until they reached New York, she decided it was safer to stay in her cabin.

Although the ship's dining room was now much emptier, the three remaining Sanderses felt no effects from the storm, showing up promptly for meals and enjoying them to the utmost.

"You know, seasickness is all in the mind," Dora said, helping herself to more English trifle from the serving bowl. "Too bad Jenny and I can't have our usual lovely evening chat."

Harry knew that Jenny wasn't feeling too deprived. She was lying on her bed, thumbing through glossy American magazines and listening to records on the phonograph, all supplied by their indulgent steward.

As soon as they reached calmer waters and were approaching New York harbor, Jenny got up early with Harry to see the *Queen Mary* arrive. It was a mild autumn day, but the Statue of Liberty was still swathed in mist as they passed her by. Jenny looked at her and thought she was both a welcoming and comforting figure to all of the arriving immigrants.

"Welcome to America, darling," Harrison said. "It's a wonderful country, and I know you're going to be very happy here." Jenny looked at him; she'd never seen him so overcome with patriotic pride. She leaned out over the rail to catch one last glimpse of the statue. She could no longer see the Atlantic Ocean, her one connection to England's shores. I just can't look in the direction of home, she thought, it makes me feel too sad and lonely. She turned to Harry and hugged him closely.

"You're always right," she said.